TERRIBLE LOVELY DEMON

AN M/M PARANORMAL ROMANCE

POSSESSIVE LOVE

ODESSA HYWELL

Printed in the United States of America.

First Printing, 2023

Author: Odessa Hywell

www.odessahywell.com

Edited and Proofread by Lynda Lamb @ Refinery Edits

Formatting by Delaney Rain Author Services

Cover art and design by Charli Childs

CONTENT WARNINGS & KINKS

CONTENT WARNINGS

Explicit Sexual Content Between a Human and a Demon, Strong Language, Childhood Cancer, Non-Human Genitalia, Medical Procedures, Blood, Violence, Cancer Relapse, Child Abuse, Temporary Main Character Death.

KINKS

Snowballing, Cum Play, Felching, Switching, Marking, Tail Play, Double Penetration

ACKNOWLEDGMENTS

As always, thank you to my wonderful editor Lynda. She's edited nearly every book I've written since 2021. I'm so grateful that she makes time for me, even when times are difficult for me.

The same can be said for Laura, my tried and true alpha reader. Even when she's not fond of a particular book, her feedback has always been helpful—whether I ignore it or not. Sometimes, you need someone to tell you what you don't want to better know what you do.

Terrible Lovely Demon's list of Content Warnings and Kinks are thanks to Lindsey [coffee_and_spicy_reads]. Her feedback and input were invaluable for the development of this novel. I look forward to working with her again in the future, if she has half the mind.

To best friends.
The ones who'd summon a demon for you.
Or dispose of a body with you.

PROLOGUE

E veryone dies.

It's a not-so-little-known fact of life.

Everyone dies.

Some people are just dying a lot sooner than most people. By some people, I mean me. By most people I mean—

The heavy door that controls entry into my stale hospital room swings open and slams against the ugly cream walls with a loud bang. It sways slowly shut as my best friend stumbles over his feet and crashes into the side of my bed.

A manic grin twists his mouth and his eyes glint in the soft yellow overhead light. "Let's summon a demon!"

Uh.

I blink.

What?

Maybe I misheard? It wouldn't be the first time. Might be one of the last...

"Why does your face look like that?" Leland climbs onto the bed, pushing me over so he has room to curl against my side, a tiny ball of warmth to ward off the chill that has seeped into my bones over the last few months.

I could ask him the same thing. At least I have an excuse for the way I look. This is my face when I'm face to face with stupidity, which—with him as my best friend—is more often than most people.

"Stop it with the eyebrows."

He grabs a pillow from the end of the bed and slaps me with it—lightly. Of course it's a love tap, not the kind of hit he would've delivered in the past. He'd never forgive himself if I died prematurely because of him instead of the cancer currently ravaging my body.

I would forgive him for sending me to the grave slightly ahead of schedule. The thought of slowing wasting away over the course of three to six months is pure torture. Just slit my throat and be done with it, for fuck sake. Why drag out the inevitable?

A slow slip into the great unknown. Just what everyone wants. Of course, I can't tell Leland that. He's my best fucking friend, he would cry. Even if he lies and says he's not crying; he just has something in his eye.

I bat the pillow away and glare. "What eyebrows?"

I don't have hair-hair, much less eyebrows.

Thank you for that, modern medicine. Just what every sixteen-year-old wants—to be bald. Because, you know, having cancer isn't bad enough.

"Never mind. Stop trying to distract me. We don't have a lot of time before the night nurse makes his rounds." Leland's grin is still wild and unrestrained as he digs in his bag. "And he might be hot as sin but he's not a demon."

So...

I didn't mishear?

"*Let's summon a demon*," as if that's a totally normal, acceptable thing to shout in the pediatric cancer ward after midnight.

I'm concerned. I have questions.

Most importantly, "Are you high?"

If so... why didn't he share the good shit? Weed works a hell of a lot better than the standard opioids I'm given like clockwork by the RN on duty, but no one is willing to give a teenager those kinds of flowers. Just the ones that come in a vase with a standard greeting card that says shit like "Get well soon," or "I'm praying for you," and rot within days.

Someone isn't praying hard enough 'cause I'm not getting better, according to the doctor who spoke with me last week. It was decided by my care team the chemo is doing more harm than good. Kind of fucked up when the thing that's supposed to save your life is killing you faster than the thing it's supposed to eradicate.

Talk about bad luck.

Honestly, what's new?

Leland slaps a notebook with a brightly colored unicorn shitting rainbow marshmallows in my lap. I think I have more questions about the notebook than whatever crazy-ass plan he's cooked up.

"Read that while I set up." He climbs off my bed, all long gangly limbs and baggy clothes, messy hair and too big shoes, dragging his duct tape dumpster bag with him.

I'm gonna miss that fucking book bag when I'm dead and gone. It's the Mary Poppins Bag of book bags.

I'm going to miss Leland.

Shit. I blink back the tears.

"What exactly am I supposed to be reading?" I ask after clearing my throat, watching as he pulls chalk—bright pink, chunky sidewalk chalk, the kind you find in a value pack at Dollar General—and a salt container from his bag.

His mom is going to kill him if that's her kitchen salt. At least I'll have company in Hell.

"How to summon a demon."

Duh. Of course.

That makes perfect sense. What else would I be reading

about at three in the morning while dying of cancer when I should be sleeping?

I open the notebook and flip through the pages, really not sure what I'm seeing. A demon summoning ritual, if Leland is to be believed, but… how does he expect me to read this? It's just weird circles and lines, with letters that don't even look like letters.

How can *he* read this? Where did he even get this information—Reddit? Probably. It's Leland. He has a habit of stumbling into the dark side of the internet ass backwards.

"I think I'd rather die of cancer," I say as I slap the notebook shut.

Leland doesn't even bother to look up from the salt circle he's laying. "Not an option."

Not an option? *Not an option?*

"Do I even get a say?" I'm the one dying. I should definitely get a say in this demon summoning ritual plan of his.

"Nope. Get up." Leland tosses the bottle of salt in a chair and wipes his hands off on the back of his pants, leaving behind a dusty pink stain.

I sigh and throw the blanket off.

Summoning a demon seems as likely to work as the chemo has thus far so… fuck it, why the hell not? What do I really have to lose?

If this is what Leland needs to do to feel like he did everything within his power to help me in my last few months of life, I'm not going to deny him. But afterwards, he's getting me some goddamn chicken nuggets from McDonalds, with extra dipping sauce, since for the first time in what feels like forever I'll be able to keep them down. I want twelve of those motherfuckers.

"Stand there." He points and I carefully sway my way to the spot he indicated. Unlike everyone else in my life, he doesn't rush to my aid as if I'm incapable of walking several feet without assistance.

Thanks, Mom, but I can go to the bathroom. And wipe my ass. Alone.

He keeps a close eye on me, ready to move at a moment's notice should I look as if I'm about to fall, but that's it. For that —the way he's never treated me like I'm fragile, even when I am —I'll be eternally grateful.

"Okay? Now what?" I prop my hands on my hips and look down at the circle he's drawn. It's… fucking creepy. Symbols that make no damn sense.

Because, you know, obviously summoning a demon is a very logical, scientific process.

"If you're expecting me to do the chicken dance, I can tell you now it's not happening. I've got a few hail Satans in me at best."

Leland rolls his eyes. "Just stand there and try not to look stupid when the demon appears."

Try not to—*this motherfucker.*

"I don't have eyebrows!" I shout.

Of course I look stupid.

He waves his hand at me. "You were asleep when I visited earlier. I drew you some."

My mouth drops open. "No. You didn't."

"What? I've been practicing. Ivory showed me how to make them look real and everything."

His sister showed him how to make them—"them" being *my eyebrows*—look real?

I open my mouth and close it.

Ivory's make-up is always well done when she visits with Leland's parents. Not that they can visit often, since flights from New York to Memphis aren't exactly cheap. If she *did* show him, and he *has* been practicing, maybe he didn't make me look like Bert on Sesame Street.

Still, I glare. Has he ever heard of consent?

"We're going to talk about this later."

He shrugs. "Sure. Let me focus. Beau's going to freak if he catches you out of bed."

He's more likely to freak that Leland is here outside of visiting hours. And the salt. The salt is definitely going to warrant some side eye.

I cross my arms over my chest. "Carry on."

Leland starts… chanting. It's not *not* in English. But like… *old* English—the kind they spoke before people realized bathing at least once a week, preferably more, is a good thing.

"I don't think it's working." The familiar voice of my hot-as-sin night nurse sends a shiver down my spine.

Leland screams, stumbling into a chair. I jump and spin, catching myself on the wall—just barely—to see Beau resting against the end of my bed, his arms crossed over his chest, a half smile pulling at his mouth. I really shouldn't be surprised. He's one of the quieter staff; he slips in and out of my hospital room at all hours.

"Honestly not surprised," he carries on, as if he didn't just scare a precious few weeks off my already incredibly short life. "That's the worst summoning circle I've ever seen."

"What?" Leland's mouth opens and closes like a fish out of water.

"Is that… sidewalk chalk?" Beau pushes off the bed, approaches the circle and swipes his hand through said chalk. "Really? Sidewalk chalk." He arches an eyebrow at Leland. It's a very judgmental eyebrow. "On behalf of demons everywhere, I'm insulted."

My brain screeches to a grinding halt.

Did he just say…

"Huh?" Leland has apparently lost higher function, as well. His wide eyes drift to me before zooming back to Beau. "Did you… Are you… But… salt?"

"And you, you're a smart kid," Beau says, his gaze pinning me in place. Leland, he ignores.

I'm really starting to wonder if I *am* smart because I did just let my best friend attempt to summon a demon in the pediatric cancer ward, knowing full well my night nurse would be making his rounds sooner rather than later.

"Care to explain your friend's stupidity? Also—" Beau puts his hands on his hips. It's hot—the stern expression he levels at the both of us. Why is he so hot? Why am I thinking about that right now? What is wrong with me? "It's way past visiting hours." *Ha! Called it.* "And who exactly do you expect to clean up all this salt?"

I shoot Leland a nasty look. This whole endeavor was his idea but *I* have to be the one to explain our behavior. Only, I have no explanation for this.

"Are you really a demon?" Leland asks, his voice loud enough to carry into the hallway. I wince and glance at the door, glad it's closed. The last thing I want is someone overhearing this conversation. Leland won't be allowed to visit anymore if they think he's crazy. I mean, he is crazy but they don't *know* that. At least, no one has been able to confirm it. "Prove it."

"I'm a demon, not a magician," Beau says, hands still on his hips, still looming over us. Not that he can really loom. Dude didn't win in the height department. I'm taller than him at sixteen. "Do you expect me to pull a hellhound from a hat?"

I almost choke on a laugh but...

Jesus H. Christ. He's a demon. A *demon.*

Those exist? And, work in hospitals?

Is that like a vampire working at a blood bank? Or a werewolf being a park ranger? Do vampires and werewolves exist, if demons do? Shit. If they do, and I let one take a bite out of me, can I kiss cancer goodbye? Or just my life?

Leland crosses his arms over his chest. "If you're a demon, *prove it.* We want to make a deal."

Beau looks between us, his gaze deep and assessing. Then his eyes change, and they look like nothing I've ever seen before. Black, aside from green horizontal slit pupils.

"A deal?" he rasps. I shiver—and really regret not changing out of my hospital gown this afternoon after that round of tests —as a forked tongue flicks from between his lips. At least I'm wearing sweatpants.

Okay. Yeah. Demon. Maybe? He could be something besides a demon. Like… Shit. I don't know. He's definitely not human.

"I'm listening."

CHAPTER
ONE
BEAU

SOMETHING LIKE A DECADE LATER...

Humanity never ceases to astound me.

After everything—the invention of the wheel, underwater exploration, space! Humans have literally been to the moon—*the moon, for fuck sake*—and after all that, all those amazing accomplishments…

I blink at the young man standing in front of me. Open and close my mouth. What am I even supposed to say?

I've been alive a long time—millennia. Fucked a few kings. Been friends with a few queens. Fucked a few of those too, to be fair. Not many—my preference is mostly male—but still. Seen the rise and fall of empires. Been the reason a few of them rose and fell, to be honest. Actually witnessed humanity shoot for the stars and reach them—sort of.

Society has come so far since I first clawed my way out of what most people refer to as Hell, but is just the waypoint for all souls. And despite all of that…

Maybe I misheard him?

"I'm sorry. Can you repeat that?"

His cheeks turn pink. He looks away, rubbing his neck with his free hand—the one not currently stuffed into his baggy sweatpants. "I was building a Lego set at my desk and dropped the super glue in my lap."

I nod encouragingly.

Yeah. Yeah, I got that part.

He was building a Lego set and dropped super glue in his lap. It happens. No big deal. I'm not going to judge him for having shaky hands. Who hasn't dropped something before, after all?

Why he was building a Lego set with super glue is a mystery worth solving another day. It's not the most concerning part of this story.

"Some of it got on my... *my penis*—" he whispers, and swallows, eyes anywhere but on me. I lay my hand over my mouth and hum, gesturing with my other hand for him to continue with his explanation. I'm not going to laugh. Maybe. Probably. Or ask why he was naked while using super glue, because I'm a professional. Mostly. "When I went to wipe it away... It was an accident, I swear."

Yeah. No. I have no doubt it was an accident. Who willingly glues their hand to their own dick? To anyone's dick, for that matter? That's not something most people who have a penis are going to do just for the fun of it. Nothing about having your hand glued to any part of your body is fun. But glued to your penis—yeah, no.

"Okay. Do you mind if I take a look?" I reach for a pair of gloves.

His eyes widen; he shakes his head and shuffles backwards. "You? But. W-What about a-a lady nurse? No offense, but I'm not... I'm not *gay*."

"Sure." I barely manage to school my expression. It's on the tip of my tongue to offer him a sticker and congratulate him for coming out as heterosexual in the emergency department, where we treat *emergencies* regardless of race, religion, or sexual orientation. "I can ask one of my female colleagues to assist you. You'll, of course, have to explain to them the nature of your visit, and let them perform a physical exam. They'll be responsible for treatment."

"W-Wait!" He stumbles after me as I turn for the door, and I pause in removing my gloves. "Just… don't laugh."

He squeezes his eyes shut and shoves his pants down his hips. I open my mouth and close it before I ask if he thinks *I* may laugh, what made him think a *lady nurse* wouldn't?

Another mystery for another day. I turn to better inspect him.

His cock isn't anything to write home about. Not any more impressive or unimpressive than the three other cocks I've encountered this shift alone. At this point in my life, a cock is a cock and unless I'm riding it I really don't have an opinion one way or another.

His grooming routine leaves something to be desired. Probably why he decided it's better if I handle his unfortunate situation. I can't say I blame him. And on the bright side, at least his whole hand isn't attached. Just his index and middle finger, glued halfway down his shaft. The skin around them is red and irritated, probably from his attempts to unstick the digits himself.

Removal will be pretty straightforward. He could've used the internet and skipped a visit to the emergency room altogether, saved himself some embarrassment. No one would ever have known about this unfortunate incident if he had.

"Okay, Mr. Davide—let me tell you what we're going to do."

He nods and sits on the edge of the bed as I explain pure acetone will eat through the glue without harming his sensitive bits.

Sure, his dick will be a little dry afterwards but nothing a little oil-based lube can't help with. He strikes me as the kind of man who should invest in lube stock. Maybe he already has? All types pass through the ER. We treat everyone.

Once I'm sure he understands and agrees to treatment, I slip out of the private room to get a bottle of what amounts to nail polish remover from the supply closet, chuckling under my breath, while he reevaluates his life choices.

When I return after getting sidetracked by a hundred other tasks, it takes thirty minutes of careful work with a Q-tip (since pouring acetone directly on his cock isn't an option—he'll be worse off if the acetone gets in his meatus) and one unnecessary visit from the emergency department attending, who lectures Mr. Sticky Hands about safe working conditions, to free his fingers before he's able to go home. As he leaves with discharge papers in hand, one of my colleagues comes to stand at my side.

"You think he did it on purpose? So he could get some hand action?" Maddie asks, crossing her arms over her chest and rocking back on her heels as she watches him exit.

You'd be surprised how many people turn up at the emergency room for a non-emergency just so they can get their rocks off.

A frequent flier of ours accidentally-on-purpose loses things inside of himself just to have the nurse on duty fish them out. One day, he's going to shove something in his anal channel that will need to be removed surgically. I hope I'm not on shift when that day arrives. If I am, I just might quit. Assume a new identity in a different city. Won't be the first time, after all.

"Ha. Not likely," I reply as we turn towards the desk. I need to know what I'm dealing with next. Nothing serious, I hope. The last thing I want is my twelve-hour shift to turn into a fourteen-hour slog. "He requested a woman, but changed his mind fast when he realized he'd have to explain to a member of the opposite sex exactly what happened. Apparently he's not gay."

No heterosexual man's pride would survive the story Mr. Sticky Hands told me, if they had to tell it to an attractive woman. No homosexual's pride for that matter. Some things, doesn't matter who you are or who you like to fuck, are universal.

Maddie laughs, the sound at odds with the hushed, somber feel of the ER. "What exactly happened?"

"He was playing with Legos and dropped the super glue in his lap." I shake my head and grab another chart, flipping it open.

"That's a new one. He was naked?" she asks and I nod. "Stupid bastard."

I hum, my attention already on my next patient.

Maxton Grant, a twenty-five-year-old otherwise healthy male, suffering from a dog bite on his right lower leg. Not as interesting as Mr. Sticky Hands, but an easy in and out. Maybe I'll actually be out of here on time for once. Not counting on it, but a demon can hope. Not much use in praying but even the most sinful have aspirations—or, as they are better known in the emergency department, pipe dreams.

Stepping into Mr. Grant's room, I smile at the disheveled young man perched on the edge of the bed. His pant leg is rolled up, a bloody bandage wrapped around his calf muscle. "Mr. Grant—"

His mouth falls open and his eyes widen as he stumbles to his feet. "You."

"Me. Your nurse. I'm Beau. How about you sit down and I take a look at your leg?" I sit his folder on a small metal tray and grab a pair of gloves.

Most likely, a quick poke in the shoulder after I clean and dress his wound and we can have him out the door. If I take my sweet-ass time it'll be right around clock-out time when I finish.

If I manage to slip out of this level of Hell unseen, I can pick up takeout on the way home, preferably something fast and greasy, and bolt my door behind me. A solid twelve hours of peace, away from humanity, is just what every demon needs after a long day of pretending to be human.

I can already taste the fast-food burger and fries on my

tongue. Shit. Maybe I'll get a milkshake while I'm at it. A little indulgence won't kill me.

"You… You don't remember me?" Mr. Grant asks.

I pause beside him, searching his face. He's young and handsome, obviously in good health. Stubble covers his wide jaw and sharp chin. High, flushed cheekbones lend him an air of refinement. His eyes are bright in the overhead light. They glow, but not from fever.

He's not a man I'd mind taking to bed. Maybe I have. But no, he's far too young to be anyone I slept with recently.

With the work I do, humans come and go so often it's impossible to remember them all—bed partners or not. Maybe I treated him in the past. He's not someone I've dealt with unofficially in a hospital setting. I'd recognize his soul if that was the case.

"I'm sorry. I'm horrible with names and faces. They all tend to blur together after a long day." I grab a pair of scissors, drop to my knees beside the bed and begin snipping away at the bandages.

"You haven't changed. At all," he mutters. I glance up to find his eyes pinned on me. They're a pretty, soft brown. The eyes of a kind man, a kind soul. No doubt if we struck a deal, once it was fulfilled his soul would sustain me for decades. But Maxton Grant doesn't have the look of a man who'd make a deal with a demon. "It's been…"

He swallows and fists the sheet. His knuckles turn white.

I carefully peel the bandage from his leg.

The bite isn't bad. Bloody, but not deep.

"Almost… Almost ten years. St. Jude's Hospital in Memphis, Tennessee. You… You…"

He squeezes his eyes closed and I sit back as he struggles to breathe. His chest heaves as he wheezes. The sound is loud in the otherwise silent room.

Once upon a time, I did work there. But years blur for me the same way names and faces do. I've forgotten more years than most people could possibly hope to live. It's just easier that way—forgetting. Remembering people and places can be hard when your time is limitless and the people around you, people you often grow to care for, are susceptible to the corrosion of time.

Clearly, I have forgotten something of vital importance to this young man.

I lay my hand on his knee and squeeze. "Mr. Grant?"

His eyes snap open. His gaze pins me in place. "*I'm a demon, not a magician.*"

I suck in a sharp breath. The memory hits me hard and fast.

Late at night. Past visiting hours.

A cheap pink chalk summoning circle.

Two teenage boys—one of whom was him.

One demon—me.

CHAPTER
TWO

MAXTON

T en years ago I was dying of a rare form of aggressive cancer with—like most childhood cancers—no known cause. Then, suddenly, I wasn't, because of this… demon. And he doesn't remember me.

How is that possible? He saved my life.

Should I be insulted that I'm so forgettable?

I swallow past the lump in my throat as Beau reaches for my leg again with shaky hands. His cheeks are flushed pink. Clearly, seeing me after all this time has affected him on some level. The last thing I intended to do is upset him.

"Beau…" I don't know what to say.

Should I thank him for saving my life? And for those long weeks before I knew he was a demon, where he played nursemaid on nights when I spent more time bent over a toilet than in an actual bed?

I hadn't before. There hadn't been an opportunity, not with my family and doctors swarming my room as I slowly got better, asking a dozen questions I had no way to answer without exposing Beau, Leland and myself. Who would believe me and Leland if I said I made a deal with a demon?

There were times, when I was still mostly sick but improving, I didn't believe it either. But that's what happened.

My eternal soul—or, I think it was my soul, at least; the terms weren't exactly clear—in exchange for good health. Not just a cure for the cancer either—*good health*.

In the last ten years, I haven't had so much as a runny nose or cough. When everyone else is getting the flu or whatever new virus is floating around, I never worry. My immune system, for a former cancer kid—for *anyone*—is impressive.

Beau takes a deep breath and looks up. Blonde hair falls across his forehead. His eyes are a startling shade of green, nothing like the horizontal slits from that night. He's as hot now as he was then. "How have you been, Maxton?"

I exhale. "Good. Really good. Thanks to you."

He looks away before grabbing what amounts to a water bottle with a nozzle, presumably to flush out my wound. I reach out slowly and grasp his shoulder. He freezes under my hand, muscles bunching tight, as his eyes lift to meet mine.

"Seriously. Thank you. Can... Can I take you for coffee or something sometime?"

"Coffee?" He blinks and his brow furrows. "That's not necessary."

Maybe not. Maybe he doesn't require anything, even my gratitude, since he did presumably get my soul out of the bargain we struck. But I still want to take him for coffee, or... or dinner. Something. Anything. I don't want him to disappear like he did when I was a teenager.

"When does your shift end?"

He glances at the clock on the wall. "Soon."

"So when we finish up here, I'll wait for you outside. Coffee? You like coffee, right?"

There's a decent place a few blocks from the hospital. I'll buy him a cup and we can talk. Not just about that night either. I'm curious as to how he's been this last decade.

Is he curious about me at all?

Probably not. He didn't even remember me.

Beau laughs, the sound somewhat uneasy, as he starts to carefully wash the bite on my leg. The water is cool and his hands are gentle. His hands have always been soft—sure but careful and caring. "I work in an emergency room. What do you think?"

"Nurse is an interesting career choice."

He's a demon. Why work in a hospital, helping people? He could be doing... literally anything, I assume. Does he even need to work?

"Not really when you think about it. Hospitals are full of desperate people willing to do anything for just a little more time, or improved quality of life—for themselves or a loved one. Desperate people are more likely to do dumb shit."

Dumb shit like make a deal with a demon? Kind of like I did.

He runs a clean cloth over the bite and I suck in a sharp breath before clenching my jaw.

"Almost done," he mutters, squeezing the back of my leg with his free hand. "How did this happen anyway?"

"You remember Leland?" I ask.

He laughs softly and shakes his head. "Your ballsy best friend who drew a shitty summoning circle in cheap chalk and demanded I prove myself? Yeah. I remember him."

Should I be offended that he remembers Leland so easily but didn't recognize me?

"He runs an animal rescue now. I help out sometimes." A protective bitch we were sent to remove from a neglectful home —along with her pups—got mean. Not the first time it's happened. Usually Leland is the one getting a chunk taken out of him. I suppose it was only a matter of time before I was on the receiving end of an angry dog's bite.

"It's not as bad as it could've been. Once I clean and

bandage the wound, I'll give you a shot and send you home with some antibiotics."

Antibiotics. Are those even necessary? Is the shot, for that matter?

"What are the chances I get an infection?" I ask, looking down at the wound.

He looks up, a small smile pulling at his mouth. My stomach clenches and I swallow. Shit. He's still so fucking hot. "You? None."

"The deal we made…" I pluck at the thin sheet I'm sitting on as I look away. There are a dozen questions I want to ask but where do I start? Will he even answer?

He said desperate people do dumb shit all the time. I had been desperate, in my own way. Before Leland burst into my room I honestly thought I was going to die in that fucking hospital before I'd even had my first kiss.

"Having regrets?" Beau asks as he slathers an ointment over the bite.

I shake my head. "No. I'm grateful for everything you did for me but…" I trail off, attempting to gather my thoughts. Beau silently wraps my leg as he waits. "You never specified a time limit. How long until you… collect. Just—" I lean in and lower my voice, "my soul in exchange for good health."

He hums. "Something like that."

Something like that. *Something like that?*

"What does that mean?" It was my soul he accepted in exchange, right? Otherwise…

He stands, pulls his gloves off and tosses them in the trash before turning to face me again. "You still want to get that coffee?"

"Yes." We can get a coffee and talk about… everything. His place of employment probably isn't the best location to discuss our shared past.

"Here." He digs in his pocket and pulls out his phone. "Put

your number in. My shift might run late so I'll text you for a better time."

I take his phone and do as he asks. And maybe I'm an asshole for doing it but I immediately open a new message thread and text myself so I have his number too.

When my phone dings in my pocket, he shakes his head, a small smile playing at his mouth, and takes his phone back. "Don't trust me, Maxton?"

I open and shut my mouth.

How can I answer that? What does he expect me to say? He's a demon. I shouldn't trust him. But Beau wasn't just a demon ten years ago. He's not just a demon now.

He's the nurse who cared for me on the bad days my family wasn't there for, that I didn't want them there for. He helped me in and out of the shower, washed me when I couldn't do it myself, never once mentioning how malnourished I looked when I went days without eating, or the spontaneous erection I got as he rubbed lotion on my dry, cracked skin when I couldn't be bothered because what was the fucking point? I was dying regardless.

Beau made sure my favorite Jell-O was on my lunch tray every day, even when I couldn't stomach food, and sometimes snuck me a milkshake because even though we both knew it wouldn't stay down, it would at least taste just as good coming up. He *cared* far more than his job required. I was half in love with him for that alone. Then, he saved my life.

"I don't not trust you," I finally say.

He tucks his phone in his pocket. "I'll get your shot and discharge paperwork. Just hang out for a minute."

I nod and he slips out of the room. As soon as the door slides shut behind him, I reach for my phone. The first thing I do is add his number to my contacts.

Beau Holland.

Is that even his real name?

The second thing I do is open my messages with Leland. Between us, it's a lot of memes and dumb shit. Our friendship hasn't really evolved over the years. Why fix what isn't broken?

MAXTON

I'm almost done here.

LELAND

No stitches?

MAXTON

Nah. Just cleaned and bandaged the bite. I'm getting a tetanus shot too.

Also, do you remember that nurse—the not-a-magician?

He works here, in the ER.

My phone rings, but I decline the call.

Now is *not* the time to be on the phone with Leland. His loud-ass mouth will be heard down the hallway whether he's on speaker or not.

LELAND

Answer your phone!

You can't tell me something like that and not answer your phone!

MAXTON

I can't talk about him here. He'll be back with my shot and paperwork.

We're supposed to get coffee at some point.

LELAND

You invited him out for coffee?

Or did he invite you out?

MAXTON

I asked him. He gave me his phone number though.

LELAND

I have complicated feelings about this.

MAXTON

Keep them to yourself.

LELAND

Maybe they should admit you. Delirium is a symptom of a larger issue.

I laugh just as the door slides open and Beau steps back in.

"It might be a minute before your paperwork is ready but I've got your shot here. Which arm do you prefer? Still your left?"

I nod and hold out my arm.

How can he forget me but remember which arm I prefer to get jabbed in?

"Just a little poke. Deep breath," Beau says after he cleans the surface area.

Our eyes meet and we laugh.

"I'm all grown up now, you know?"

"I noticed," he says as he sinks the needle in. I peer up at him.

"If you don't text me, I want you to know I really am thankful for what you did. Not just making me better but before that. I remember how kind you were. When everything sucked, you didn't. You—"

I look away, clear my throat, and blink back the sudden tears that burn my eyes. I meet his gaze. He deserves to know how much having him look after me during the worst time of my life meant, and I should look at him when I say it. "You made dying easier. And for that alone I'll always be thankful, Beau."

Beau's green eyes latch onto mine. They're as warm and kind as I remember. For a moment, it's like I'm back in that shitty hospital room and he's leaning over my bed, asking me how he can help as I choke on tears. Of course, he couldn't. Or, at the time, I didn't know he could. All I asked was if he'd hold my hand. He did. Every single time.

"I'll text you. It might be a few days but I will."

That's the best I can hope for right now.

T wo days after treating Maxton Grant for a minor bite wound, I finally have time for a coffee. The conversation he wants to have isn't safe to have in public —humanity as a collective whole may never be ready to know about the things that go bump in the night—so a coffee shop is out of the question. We agree to meet at the park across town.

This time of day, it's mostly empty. Maxton is sitting on a bench holding two coffees when I park and turn off my car. He smiles, a nervous twitch of his lips, as he stands to meet me.

Like I told him, he's grown up a lot from that sick teenager who would quietly cry late at night after his family and friends had gone home. Not only is he taller, but he's filled out—wide shoulders, strong arms, and a trim, healthy waistline. I hardly recognize him with hair and eyebrows not drawn on by Leland.

My stomach rolls as I approach.

How am I supposed to explain myself? What happened that night?

Ten years ago, I had very carefully avoided saying anything that implied his soul was mine to collect after a specified time, and he hadn't explicitly offered it, so technically, his soul is safe and sound, far out of my reach. What we did amounted to a pinky promise. A handshake between a human and a demon. An agreement that, to the best of my knowledge, had never been made by any other demon before. Or since.

It would've been so much easier to brush him off. Pretend I didn't have a clue who he was when he recognized me. Why didn't I do that? It's not as if I owe him anything. The nature of our agreement means he owes me, not that I ever intend to collect. So what am I doing here?

"I wasn't sure you'd text," he says, holding out a coffee as I step onto the walking path.

I accept it with a small shrug. "I said I would."

And like most demons, I'm not a liar. We love to exploit loopholes but we don't lie. There's a certain pleasure in collecting a soul from a human who is fully aware of what they're agreeing to, but agrees anyway.

"Should we…" Maxton gestures to the path.

I nod and we fall into step beside one another. The silence drags but Maxton is the one who wants to have this conversation, I'm just along to answer any questions he may have. So I wait for him to break it.

It takes several minutes but eventually he blows out a slow breath and glances at me. "How have you been? I never saw you again after that night…"

"I don't typically make deals with children." I never make deals with children, in fact, but he doesn't need to know that. Yet. Eventually, I need to assure him his soul is safe. "So I thought it was best to move on before either you or Leland decided to talk."

"I didn't! We didn't," Maxton rushes to assure me, his voice rising and falling. "To be honest, even after seeing… you? Your face?" He shakes his head and I hide my grin behind a sip of coffee. At most, he saw my eyes and tongue. "Anyway, I wasn't sure anything had changed. I still felt like me—not, um… soulless. Then I started to get better."

. . .

"IN EXCHANGE FOR GOOD HEALTH, *he'll give you…" Leland trails off and glances at Max, confusion written all over his face.*

"Well?" I ask. Neither of them seems to know what comes next. Not surprising considering the chalk and salt. It's classic Leland to attempt to summon a demon but get tripped up when a demon appears. Leap long before he looks. One day, he's going to end up with broken legs. Or dead.

"I'm supposed to offer my soul, right?" Max asks as he plays with his bottom lip. His wide eyes lock on me. "Or, um… what about an I owe you? A favor?"

A favor.

A human boy indebted to a demon.

That could come in handy one day.

For what, I don't know, but I'll figure something out.

"Okay. I accept your terms."

"HOW WELL DO you remember our deal, Maxton?"

"You know you can call me Max. Like you used to." He bumps his shoulder against mine before clearing his throat and quickly stepping away. "No one really calls me Maxton except my mom. And, I remember. My soul. Or a favor, in return for good health. But you never said which, just um—" He turns pink and sips on his coffee.

The deal had been sealed with a kiss, as is standard. His first kiss, if the way he'd frozen under my mouth and made a squeak of surprise as my split tongue pressed between his lips had been any indication. I'd kept it brief, and been sure not to touch him anywhere else. Nothing about kissing him had been sexual for me. If his flushed cheeks now are anything to go by, the same can't be said for him.

Max runs his fingers through his hair, tugging on the soft

strands before shoving his hand into his pocket. "Me and Leland, we assumed you'd come for my soul at a later date—like… like ten years, 'cause what use would you have for a favor?"

What use would I have for a favor, indeed? Truthfully, none. But a child's soul, no matter how life sustaining it may be, has always been a hard limit of mine. Demons do have morals. Some of us anyway.

"Let's sit." I motion to a bench. It's still wet from the recent rainfall. Max brushes away as much water as he can with his hand before we both drop down. His thigh presses against mine as he cups his coffee in both hands.

"I feel a little like you're about to deliver bad news." His laugh is uneasy. I hate the pinched expression on his face when he glances at me. "Is… Is my time almost up? Am I—" His voice cracks. "Am I going to get sick again?"

I shake my head and bump my shoulder against his as I smile. "No. Nothing like that. I spend a lot of time on my feet so on my days off I like to be lazy."

On my days off, I tend to stay home, half catatonic on my sofa with a mindless television show for background noise.

Max's shoulders relax. He exhales and searches my face. "You don't work with sick kids anymore?"

"No." I turn to the coffee in my hand and pick at the paper label. "You were my last. Safer that way."

He frowns. "Safer?"

Why do I feel so compelled to explain myself to this boy turned man? He's not the first human I've encountered who's been curious, who's had questions. I've never had any trouble walking away from them, disappearing and reappearing under a new identity, so why him? What makes Maxton Grant so different from everyone else?

"I have no claim to your soul," I eventually say. Max's eyes widen. "The terms of our agreement were your soul or a favor.

I'm not in the habit of collecting souls from children so…" I shrug and take a drink from my cup. The coffee is tepid and bitter. It settles sour in my stomach. I can feel Max's eyes on the side of my face like a powerful laser beam.

"Beau." Max lays his hand on my thigh and I look at him. His eyes are soft in the morning light, like melted chocolate with hints of caramel. "Thank you—really. Anything you want, just ask." His lips tip at the corners. "Aside from my soul, which it seems you have no interest in. Should I be offended? Is something wrong with my soul?"

I laugh, the sound sudden and abrupt.

Is something wrong with his soul?

Who asks a demon that?

"No. Your soul is as it should be."

He blows out a breath and sits back. "That's good to know. But none of that explains why it's safer you don't work with sick kids anymore. Giving them a second chance at life can't be a bad thing…" His brows pull together as he looks at me. "Can it?"

I sit back and our shoulders brush. "It's… complicated."

He turns, just slightly, his arm sliding along the back of the bench. "I have time."

"Maybe I just don't want to explain."

Max tips his head to the side, his hair falling into his eyes before he nods. "Fair enough. You don't owe me an explanation. I know if you're not making deals with children you have a good reason. You may be a demon but you're not an asshole."

I huff and tip my coffee back, finishing the last of it before setting the cup on the bench. How does he know I'm not an asshole? Why does he have to be so understanding? Why not just demand answers like everyone else? It makes it a lot harder to keep secrets when he's so… kind.

"Children aren't capable of comprehending what making a deal with a demon really means. They're easy pickings and I

29

prefer a challenge. But you…" I glance away, not sure how to finish my thought.

"What?"

Max leans in until his chest is resting against my shoulder. The heat of his body seeps into mine and it's a struggle not to lean into him. What is it about this man I'm so drawn to? Even when he was a sick teenager I took notice of him.

"I used to hear you crying at night, after everyone had gone home, you know?" My voice is barely louder than a whisper as I curl my fingers together. "I'd stand outside your door and think how unfair it was. And I know, a lot of kids were—*are* suffering but… and maybe it makes me the asshole you're so sure I'm not, but they didn't bother me, not like seeing you so sick." I glance at Max and meet his patient gaze. "I wanted to help you, Max."

I wanted to help him so fucking badly I did the unthinkable. Something no other demon would dare do. But to do what I did —letting him drain me of every drop of magic I possess—would have been worth it, if he got to live.

His fingers brush over my shoulder and I look away again as something warm settles in my stomach. "When Leland said you wanted to make a deal, I was torn. Mostly because here was my chance to help you, give you the chance to live a long, happy life but… taking your eternal soul…"

I blow out a breath and shake my head. There's so much to explain for him to really understand why making a deal with him —with any man, woman or child—is complicated, and I'm not really sure where to start.

Max's breath is warm on my cheek before his lips settle against my flesh. Lightning crackles down my spine. He lingers before pulling back and I peek at him from the corner of my eye; his cheeks are flushed a soft pink. He clears his throat as his gaze drops.

"Thank you, Beau. For back then. And now—trying to explain all this to me even though I can tell you're struggling."

I shake my head but can't find my voice. He doesn't need to keep thanking me. Once was more than enough but Max seems determined to make sure I know how grateful he is. He doesn't even know what I had to sacrifice.

This human. What is it about him that flays me open so easily?

CHAPTER
FOUR
MAXTON

For some reason, Beau is struggling to explain what happened in my hospital room all those years ago. He's uncomfortable, and as much as I want to know exactly what happened, why he accepted a favor instead of my soul when it was up for the taking, I don't want him to disappear like he did before. If taking a step back, giving him time to take a breath and relax, will put him at ease, I'm more than willing to do that.

"Are you hungry?" I ask as I finish my coffee.

It's almost lunchtime now. I skipped out on breakfast, too nervous.

"I can always eat," Beau says.

I smile, stand up, collect our trash, and toss it into the nearby garbage bin before turning to him. "How about lunch? If you're free?"

Just because he's not working today doesn't mean I can monopolize his time. What do demons do in their free time? Make deals? Collect souls? Survive on takeout and binge watch television like the rest of us sad suckers, in between being harassed by their family and friends?

"No more demon talk?" Beau asks as he stands and pats at

his backside. If he's anything like me, the seat of his pants is a little damp. Not enough to be uncomfortable but enough to be noticeable.

I shake my head. "Nope. I still have questions but you don't have to tell me anything you don't want to. I just…"

Shit. What reason can I give for wanting to spend time with him? No way am I going to admit he's responsible for my gay awakening.

When he kissed me that night, it meant nothing to him. Just a way to seal our deal. The press of his mouth against mine lasted maybe three seconds; he didn't even pull me close enough to feel the erection I sprung just from the feel of his split tongue against mine, though if he'd bothered to look down, he'd have seen it. But for me? No other kiss since has compared.

Is that because he's a demon and we struck a deal? The forked tongue? Or because at sixteen, when I was dying, he was kind and attentive but never crossed the line, even when it was probably obvious I had a major crush on my hot-as-sin night nurse? I'd have let him take full advantage in a heartbeat.

Obviously, teenagers are dumb and can't be trusted to make smart choices. Thankfully, Beau is a decent enough guy not to take advantage of a hormonal child fighting for their life. Because, looking back now, I can admit that even though I felt grown, I was still just a kid. I had no clue how the world worked.

"I know a place you might like," Beau says.

I shove my hands into my pockets and rock back on my heels. "We can take your car."

"It's not the kind of place we can get to by driving." He offers me his hand as I frown. If we can't get there by driving, how are we getting there? Nothing that I know of is within walking distance. "Trust me?"

I meet his green eyes.

That's the second time he's asked me to do that.

This time, I won't pretend I don't.

Beau, I trust with my life. He saved it so why wouldn't I? If he wanted me dead, he could have let me die a long time ago. Unless the reason he doesn't collect souls from children is because they age like a fine wine. But no, that's not who Beau is as a... demon, person?

"Okay." I slide my hand into his. What do I have to lose, after all? Not my soul. Beau doesn't seem interested in it which seems very... un-demon-like.

He tugs me closer and wraps his arm around my midsection. It's kind of funny how much bigger I am than him now. I can easily tuck him under my chin. We'd line up so well. My belly clenches and I fight the urge to drag him closer, so close we merge into one person.

His hold is strong and I have no doubt he can easily subdue me if I do anything he doesn't like. Perks of being a demon, maybe? I still don't want to upset him or make him uncomfortable.

"Deep breath," he says. I inhale sharply and feel a tug just below my ribcage. My feet leave the ground and everything is dark for a second. The world seems to spin. My knees buckle and I stumble; Beau's grip tightens as he holds me steady. "Easy. First time is always rough."

"What was that?" I ask before my gaze is caught by a man walking past us, his expression bored, as if people appearing out of thin air is an everyday occurrence. He's... he's beautiful.

Inhuman.

Holy shit. He's not human.

The almost translucent wings fluttering on his back match the pale pink hair that sways around his waist. His skin is iridescent.

"Where are we? Is that a—" My voice cracks.

Beau follows my gaze. "Fae. Fairy. Best not to tangle with one."

I nod and swallow as Beau releases me. A fairy. My knees

knock together and I shove my fingers into my pockets to hide their shaking.

"Are we… Is this Earth?"

It's not like any place on Earth I've ever seen. The roads are cobblestone. The buildings are a mashup of medieval and modern. And I've never seen so much foliage in a city in my life. Trees spring up between buildings. Flowers are in full bloom alongside the walkways. Vines are climbing every structure. It's wild and beautiful.

Beau tips his hand side to side as I draw my gaze away from our surroundings. "Mostly. This is Outer Banks. It's kind of like the Bermuda Triangle before the mystery was solved."

Wait. I peer down at him. The mystery of the Bermuda Triangle was solved? When? How? I have even more questions than before.

"Come on." Beau laughs under his breath and wraps his hand around my upper arm, giving me a soft tug. I stumble over my feet as I follow. "It's easier to show you than explain."

Just for the record, I'd also really like the explanation. Not just about this place—Outer Banks—but the Bermuda Triangle as well. Leland will lose his mind when I tell—Shit. Can I tell Leland?

"How does this place even exist?" I drag my feet, head on a swivel as I try to take everything in, Leland forgotten for the moment.

There are people who look like humans but others, like the Fae, who look nothing like a human.

A man with long, pointed ears and hair that gleams in the sun, wearing a crown of flowers and robes decorated in silver and green chatting to a woman dressed similarly. A short, plump woman with a beard and hands like hammers in a pair of jeans and a dirty t-shirt eating meat from a stick. She's wearing more precious gems than I've ever seen behind glass at a high-end jewelry store.

"Magic," Beau says. I open my mouth, so many questions just begging to be asked. I'm not even sure where to start. He shakes his head with a soft laugh before I can ask any of them. "Don't ask me for the details because I don't really know."

How can he not know?

"All I can tell you is Outer Banks exists on a powerful ley line," he continues, hand still steady on my arm as he leads the way. "It acts as a cloak of sorts. Humans can't see or find this place, not on their own. Those who accidentally wander too close get confused and end up stumbling around blindly until they find civilization again."

What about the ones who never find civilization again? Do they just die in the wild?

"This is…" I have no words. Amazing doesn't seem like enough.

"Too much?" Beau asks, his hand sliding down my arm until our fingers are laced together. His worried eyes meet mine. "We can leave at any time. Just say the word."

I shake my head and squeeze his hand. "No. No." The last thing I want to do is go our separate ways. I want to spend as much time with Beau as he'll allow. "We're supposed to be getting lunch, right? You said there's a place I might like?"

"It's this way." Beau takes a couple steps and turns down a hidden alleyway. Halfway down, I inhale deeply because… *holy shit*. Instead of the scents normally associated with an alley, this smells like all my favorite foods.

"What is that?" Can I have it?

"What does it smell like to you?" Beau asks as we step out of the alley. The smell is stronger now. I inhale again, sucking the scent deep into my lungs with a soft groan.

"Alfredo pasta. Parmesan chicken. Garlic bread. Cheesecake but with… raspberry sauce and caramel?" My stomach growls and I lay my hand on top of it. I didn't realize I was so hungry. It feels as if I haven't eaten in days, but I had dinner last night.

"Here." Beau stops and pulls open a door; saliva pools in my mouth as I step through and my senses are assaulted by all the scents, sounds and sights.

There are a dozen or more long tables. People—some of whom look more human than others—are seated shoulder to shoulder, talking and laughing as they devour the meal in front of them. No one even glances our way.

"Welcome to I Know a Guy," a young man with lavender hair says, his wings fluttering behind him, feet a good half foot off the ground. It's rude to stare but I can't help it. "Just the two of you?"

"Just us," Beau says, laying his hand on my spine as I gape at the flying impossibility who turns and inspects the dining room before whipping back around, a sharp-toothed smile in place.

"Fourth table down. Food will be out shortly."

But… we didn't order anything?

Beau tugs and I follow mindlessly, eyes everywhere and nowhere at once. I assume we're at the right table when Beau pulls me down on the bench to sit beside him. The guy to my left shuffles but we're still pressed together from shoulder to hip. Personal space isn't a concept here.

When I look at him, his eyes are yellow and glowing. "First time?"

I nod dumbly, unable to find the words.

He peeks around me and nods to Beau, who bumps his shoulder against mine. "You alright?"

"I… I don't know. This is…" I'm sitting between a demon and a… a something. There's a not-quite-human girl across from us, happily devouring a plate full of meat—bones and all. Beside her is a girl who looks to be human, enjoying a plate of nothing but dessert.

"We can leave anytime you want." Beau's breath is warm on my cheek; his hand is steady on my back.

I shake my head. The last thing I want to do is leave. No, I want to ask questions and learn more about this place, these… people. Beau.

"Make room," a lyrical voice says just behind us. Beau leans away and a plate is placed in front of me. I gape at the contents. Alfredo pasta, parmesan chicken, garlic bread and a small slice of cheesecake with raspberry sauce and caramel drizzle. Just like I smelled in the alley on the way here.

What in the…

I glance at Beau's plate. Steak, mashed potatoes, roasted vegetables, a yeast roll, and banana pudding.

"How did…"

He unwraps the roll of utensils our server left behind and shrugs, seemingly unconcerned about a meal he didn't order being delivered only moments after we arrived. "Magic."

Okay. Yeah. Magic. If magic can give me my favorite food anytime I want, sign me up. I am all for magic.

CHAPTER
FIVE
BEAU

F ood has a way of bringing people from all backgrounds together.

Minutes ago, Max was wide eyed and uneasy in a room full of paranormal creatures (and their human companions). Now he's devouring the food on his plate as if he hasn't eaten in days, or weeks.

Probably because the Fae and humans who own and operate I Know a Guy don't just give a person whatever meal they're craving at the time. They deliver the best tasting version of that meal. And their specialty? Human food.

"Want more?" a young elf asks from directly over Max's shoulder. He startles so hard the last bite of cheesecake drops from his fork into his lap. He stares at it long and hard before scooping it up with his finger and popping it into his mouth. He blushes when he notices me watching. I honestly can't blame him. He isn't the first and won't be the last person to do the same.

"Thank you. But we're good," I tell the server as I attempt to smother my grin. She takes our empty plates and leaves as quickly and as silently as she appeared. "How was it?"

Max wipes his mouth with a napkin and shifts. He can't

possibly sit any closer. We're pressed together from shoulder to ankle but I don't mind the closeness at all. The heat of his body is kind of nice. He'd be a lot warmer with a little less clothes. I can ensure it.

"Nothing is ever going to taste better, is it?" Max reaches for his glass of wine.

I hmm. "Probably not. But anytime you want to come back, I'll bring you. You'll never order because they'll always know exactly what will hit the spot, which is part of the charm."

"Everyone here is… I uh—" Max rubs the back of his neck after setting his glass down, a pink flush darkening his cheeks. He looks around before lowering his eyes and looking at me through his lashes. "I don't know the polite term. Supernatural? Paranormal? Inhuman? I don't want to insult anyone."

Has he always been this accepting? This fucking sweet? Probably. Max is a good soul—a truly good one. If I ever made a deal for it—which I would never—the collection would give me a magic high that would make every other demon I encountered for the next hundred years jealous.

"Supernatural is a good catchall. Though, some prefer parahuman." I tell him as the Fae who told us where to sit appears over his shoulder, holding out a ticket that I accept. "And this restaurant caters to both humans and supernaturals."

We stand and I lay my hand on Max's back, guiding him towards the exit as he continues to look around. If he doesn't have anywhere to be, we can explore Outer Banks. The food isn't even the best part of this supernatural safe haven. Though, it is a pretty impressive part.

"I know a guy!" Max grins. It's wide and happy as his eyes dance with excitement, and he wiggles under my hand. "Because you have to know a guy to get here—to Outer Banks—right?"

A number of parahumans laugh under their breath, not that he can hear them. He's not the first person to be slow on the uptake. He won't be the last.

"Pretty much. You want to explore some before I take you home?" I hold gold coins out to the dwarf behind the checkout counter.

"Can we?" Max asks, the words jumbling together in his enthusiasm. He's like a child just given chocolate for the first time. His happiness does something to me. Warms me from the inside out.

There was a time when I didn't think I'd ever see him truly happy—he was dying, and I was unable to help—so now, I want to do everything I possibly can to keep him smiling. He has a beautiful smile—always has. The way it lights him up could illuminate a city.

The dwarf bites each coin before dropping them into a safety deposit box. "Enjoy your day."

I slide my hand into Max's and pull him out the door. There's so much I want to show him, and the best place to start—"How about we check out the shopping district?"

His hand squeezes mine. "Okay."

I lead him down the street—past a couple of small food places that cater to a more specific diet, for a more specific clientele—before we slip into another alleyway.

On the other side, we join a crowd of afternoon shoppers. None of them pay us any attention as they head towards their next destination; it's not unusual to see a human here, though they are always accompanied by someone inhuman.

"This is amazing," Max whispers, his eyes wide and darting from one place to the next, never stopping long enough to really take anything in. His hand tightens around mine and he steps closer, until we're pressed together. "I don't know what anything is but it's… it's amazing."

I grin and bump my shoulder against his. "See anything you want to explore?"

The variety of businesses is wide.

Occult shops offering a selection of wares depending on what you want or need. An apothecary run by a green witch who can cure any number of ailments suffered by supernatural and human alike. (Not cancer, sadly. I asked a long time ago.) A salon staffed by an elf with the most amazing hair. A Fae who offers gleamers for a steep price. Boutiques that sell clothing imbued with magic. Jewelers who specialize in precious gems and rare metals. Whatever Max wants to see, I have the time to show him.

He points to a shop down the street—The Bone Tarot. "What's that?"

"An occult shop. They offer tarot and palm readings, among other things. The witch who owns it is a medium."

He blinks slowly as he opens and closes his mouth. "Can they talk to ghosts?"

I nod. "You want to check it out?"

Max swallows. "Maybe? Yeah? Is that okay?"

I pull him across the street towards the shop. The door opens as I reach for the knob and we step inside. It's bright and colorful, filled with books and other powerful items. Magic hums in the air.

A young woman wearing a flowing yellow sundress with a leather jacket and biker boots is seated on the counter, reading a book. She puts it down as the door snaps shut behind us.

"Welcome to The Bone Tarot. Interested in a palm reading?" Her boots thump against the hardwood floor and her dress swirls around her knees as she lands on her feet.

"You want one?" I ask Max.

"Um…" He chews his bottom lip.

She holds her hand out, an encouraging smile tugging at the corner of her mouth. "First one is on the house."

I nudge him forward. "Go for it."

He looks at me before stepping toward the young woman and offering her his hand. She flips it over and looks down at his palm.

A slow smile brightens her face as she drags her finger over his skin. "This is your life line. Do you see the break? Here, you had a close encounter with death. You were young—a teenager?"

Max exhales heavily and nods, peeking at me. "I had cancer as a kid."

"Rough. But look at you now." She runs her finger over another section of his palm. "You'll never be good at sports but you're full of energy, and will live a long, fulfilled life. And here, this is your love line. You'll have a happy love. Sweet. Understanding. A forever kind of love. Soulmates. A fated love. You've already met them."

The witch tips his hand just slightly. "Your fate line is clear and straight. A good and lucky future. Stable." She cups his hand in hers and shuts her eyes. "Intelligent and adaptable, you're curious and creative—good with your hands, a fixer of broken things—but should really use more moisturizer."

I laugh under my breath. The apothecary just down the street will carry a good lotion. We can buy some.

She lets him go and I lay my hand on Max's back. He leans into my touch as he peers down at his hand with a slightly mystified look, as if he's wondering how she could know all that just by inspecting his palm. "Thank you, I think?"

"What about you?" she asks with a hopeful smile. I shake my head and lay a gold coin on the counter. The first palm reading may have been free but she clearly expected to make a sale of some sort. I don't need anything she's offering, but a small tip for the service she did provide isn't unwarranted.

"Have a good day." I take Max's hand, the one he's not currently staring at, and guide him towards the door. It opens and shuts behind us. "Let's go to the apothecary."

His thick brows furrow. "That's like a pharmacy, right?"

"Pretty much." The remedies are herbal. Never mind the touch of magic that makes them more effective. "They'll have a good lotion."

He looks down at his hand again, flexing his fingers as he

does so. "She could tell I was sick as a kid." His brown eyes lift to meet mine. "Do you think she knows you… saved me?"

I shrug as I look away. "Only she can say. Every witch has different knowledge and skills."

Maybe she did know. Maybe not. Either way, we'll never know. It hardly matters in the long run what she knows about either of us, she won't tell us—or anyone else, for that matter—without asking for payment.

Max is silent as we continue towards the apothecary. I can feel his gaze on the side of my face but I don't say anything as he looks his fill. "Can… Can people tell that you're… you?"

I laugh under my breath. Can they tell I'm me? "They know I'm not human, but I'm using a glamor so they don't know I'm a demon."

"A glamor?" Max's brows furrow again.

"It's what makes me appear human." It's not like I can walk around with misshapen eyes, a forked tongue, horns, and all the other features that mark me as inhuman. Actual humans who don't know about the parahuman community would run screaming in the other direction. Before returning with holy water and torches. Neither would do a whole lot of damage but the experience would be traumatizing all around.

Max comes to a stop. He inspects me from head to toe. "Can I see?"

I swallow. "See what?"

But I don't need to ask what he wants to see. I already know. "You."

"Oh. Um." Is it a good idea to show him what I look like under the blonde hair and green eyes? He probably won't be so willing to hold my hand afterwards. Our developing friendship could end from one second to the next, and that's the last thing I want. Right now, Max can trick himself into believing I'm human. But once I shed the face he has come to know and trust…

Is it selfish to want to stay hidden so I can spend a little more time with him? Maybe find out what about him calls to something deep inside of me?

"Please, Beau?" He squeezes my hand; his brown eyes search my face, as if by looking hard enough he'll see through my glamor. "I… I want to know you. *The real you.*"

I sigh. I'm such a pushover where Max is concerned. Anyone else I'd tell to go fuck themselves, but for him, I'm so agreeable. If any of my supernatural friends find out, I'll never live it down. Yet I can't bring myself to care. "If you're sure?"

Max nods. "I'm sure. Here?"

I shake my head. "No. Let's find somewhere less crowded."

"Do you…" He sinks his teeth into his bottom lip and drops his gaze. The soft flush that tints his cheeks makes my fingers itch. I want to reach out and stroke it so badly. "We could go to my place? Or yours?"

"Yours is better."

If he freaks out, it's best we're alone. And somewhere I can flee but know he's safe.

CHAPTER
SIX
MAXTON

Did I wash last night's dinner dishes? Or are they sitting beside the sink like a neglected child? There are definitely clothes piled up in the chair in the living room because I couldn't be bothered to fold them last night. Or at any point since I washed them three days ago.

What about my lube? Shit. Did I put it away after I jerked off on the sofa thinking about a certain demon? Probably not. Just my luck. In my defense, I didn't think I'd be bringing Beau home with me today.

He's standing to the side, slightly behind me while I unlock my apartment.

"I'm sorry about the mess," I say as soon as we step inside and I shut the door. "It's not usually like this I swear."

His laugh is uneasy. I look at him. He's been nervous since I asked to see him—the real him. But he said yes.

"Considering our history, do you really think I care about clothes and lube?"

My cheeks burn and I look away.

Maybe he doesn't care, but I do.

How am I supposed to make a good impression on him if it looks as if I can't even properly care for myself or my home?

"Max." Beau lays his hand on my forearm and I glance at him. "I really don't mind but I'll wait if you want to pick up."

"Just let me…" I trail off and rush to the chair I store my clean clothes in, pick them up and shove the half empty bottle of lube in my pocket. It only takes a moment to toss the clothes into my closet, where they'll probably stay until they eventually make it into the dirty clothes. I shove the lube in the bedside table for safe keeping.

When I return, Beau is still in the living room, now standing in front of my bookshelf holding a picture frame. He glances up when I stop at his side. "I didn't think you'd want a reminder of the worst time of your life."

I reach out and take the picture.

I'm dressed in a tux—head bald, eyebrows missing, dark circles under my eyes, rail thin—standing in front of a wall painted with a dozen different zoo animals. Leland is in a tux too, handsome as ever. His arm is tossed around my neck, head thrown back as he laughs. Beau is just inside the frame wearing a suit jacket over scrubs, a half smile on his face as he peers at the pair of us with what I've always thought of as affection.

"I thought it was dumb—having a mock prom for cancer kids. Leland didn't give a shit what I thought. There was free food and if I didn't eat mine, he would. He did too. And got sick everywhere. You remember?"

His smile is soft and fond. "I remember."

"It was a good night." I shrug as I set the picture back on the shelf. "We needed those moments of normalcy to remind us there was something worth fighting for, a life after the pain and suffering." He lays his hand on my back and I lean into the supportive touch. "Plus, it's the only picture I have of you. I have group pictures with my care team but you're never in them."

Beau looks away. "I try to avoid having my picture taken. It's not really possible these days with ID needed for everything and cameras everywhere, but intentional photos with me in them could draw unwanted attention in the future."

In the future…

"How um… How long have you been here? Or, I guess, alive?" Is that okay to ask? Something he's comfortable sharing with me?

"A long time. The Roman Empire was an infant when I got here."

The Roman Empire.

How long ago was that again?

Beau chuckles. "Don't bother doing the math. You wanted to see me without my glamor, remember?"

I nod and step back. "Okay. I'm ready when you are."

Beau takes a deep breath.

The first thing to change is his eyes—eyes I remember vividly. His forked tongue flicks out the same way it did that night as a pair of black horns appears on his head. They curl backwards, almost half a foot long and ribbed. His nose and chin sharpen, not unattractively but unnaturally, as black spider veins creep along his skin.

I glance down. The dark lines cover his arms. His nails are longer now—pointed and sharp. The tips of his fingers are coal black. When I look up, his eyes and mouth are lined with the same color, as if he's been playing in a soot pile. I reach out and cup his jaw. Beau sucks in a sharp breath as I slide my hand around to grasp the nape of his neck.

"You're beautiful," I mutter as I tug him forward and brush my mouth against the corner of his. His exhale is sharp and hot on my cheek. He trembles under my hand. "Will you kiss me for real?"

"Maxton." His voice is soft. It quivers like the rest of him.

"I'm not a child anymore. And I really want you to kiss me. I need to know."

His swallow is audible. "Know what?"

"If the way I felt that night was just my imagination."

"Your imagination?" he repeats.

"Uh huh." I turn my head just enough to press our lips together lightly. "No kiss since has been as good, has made me feel the way that one did. And it wasn't even a real kiss.

"Did you know I realized I was gay that night? I suspected I was but that night confirmed it for me. *You* confirmed it for me." Beau's breathing is rapid and unsteady. "I know it wasn't like that for you. You didn't really kiss me, not because of desire. I want you to kiss me now. Please, Beau?"

"Fuck, Max." He surges forward and slots his mouth over mine as he wraps his arm around my waist. I groan and open. His tongue is hot and slick, longer than I remember, but split down the middle like I recall. The twin sides curl and twist in a way they didn't last time. I pull him into my arms before pushing my tongue into his mouth.

He melts against my chest with a soft moan, pressing his hips into mine. We're both hard. I push my leg between his thighs and he rolls his hips, riding my leg as his fingers tug on my shirt.

I'm panting for breath when I turn my head to rest my cheek against his.

"How was it?" Beau asks, voice quivering.

"Better than I remember," I rasp. This is so much more than a kiss to seal a deal between a dumb human and a lovely demon.

"Yeah?" His fingers dig into my sides. I pull back and cup his cheek, tipping his head back so I can just look at him. Anyone else seeing him like this would be horrified. He doesn't look human—not really. I don't care. All I see when I look at him is the man who showed me nothing but kindness and patience on days when I wasn't kind or patient. Maybe I have a bit of a savior complex but I can't find it within myself to care.

"I'd like to kiss you again." I drag my thumb over his cheek before catching his bottom lip. He flicks his tongue out and I catch a glimpse of pointed teeth. They look dangerous, deadly, but I'm not scared. I could never be scared of him.

His smile is slow and small but there. "Any time."

"How about now?" I ask.

Beau laughs. "What? You want to spend the day kissing me?"

I drop my hand from his face and lace our fingers together. "Yes."

As crazy as it seems, I think I want to spend the rest of my life kissing Beau.

He follows as I tug him towards the sofa. I sit and pull him into my lap. He lands with his knees on either side of my thighs as I grasp his waist and tug him against my chest.

Our mouths meet without hesitation and I slip my tongue between his lips again. Beau pushes his fingers into my hair. A sound—soft and whiny and inhuman—vibrates his throat as he rolls his hips. I'm so hard behind my zipper it hurts as I rise to meet him. He feels so good in my lap, grinding on my cock as he fists my hair. At this rate, I'm going to come in my pants like a teenager.

"Beau," I mutter against his mouth.

He hums and nips at my bottom lip before capturing my mouth once more. I slip my hand under his shirt and pause, fingering the raised lines I find. They don't feel like scars but I don't have a clue what they could be. Maybe the dark veins that extend down his arms are also hidden under his shirt.

Will he let me see if I ask?

I press a line of kisses across his jaw, towards his ear. "Can I take your shirt off?" His nails scratch over my scalp as he pulls back. I tighten my arm around him. I don't want him to move further away. "It's okay if you don't want to show me but I promise nothing I see is going to make me want to stop kissing you."

The world could be ending and I'd ignore it in favor of kissing him.

He worries his bottom lip between his sharp teeth before reaching for the hem of his shirt. I help him pull it over his head and discard it. He drops his hands to his sides, face turned away, as I run my palms up his ribcage.

The lines I felt are the spider veins. They run under his flesh the way blood vessels do.

"Doesn't change anything," I whisper as I brush my thumb over a nipple until it hardens under my touch. He whimpers and arches his back. "The missing belly button shouldn't be so surprising. I assume you weren't born like me?"

Beau shakes his head. "Demons don't reproduce, not like humans."

"I have questions, but they can wait until we're done kissing. If that's okay?"

"More than okay." His voice shakes with laughter before I slot my mouth over his to quiet the sound. He pulls back just long enough to help me out of my shirt before we come together again. His chest is warm and smooth against mine. His lips are soft, mouth hot, tongue slick.

It doesn't take long for us to fall into a comfortable rhythm. I swallow his soft moans of pleasure and toy with his nipples as he grinds against my cock. The ache in my balls that had started to recede returns full force in an instant.

"If you keep playing with my nipples," Beau gasps against my mouth, "I'm going to come."

"Seems fair—if you keep grinding on my lap, I'm going to make a mess of my boxers." He's still shifting his hips and I'm literally moments from coming. Pleasure is a hot tide washing up and down my spine.

"Should I stop?" He doesn't sound as if he wants to stop.

"As many times as I jerked off thinking about you after that first kiss I think I'm owed this orgasm. Don't you?"

He laughs and tugs my head down, bringing our lips together. I roll his nipple between my thumb and index finger, teasing the hard peak until he's moaning into my mouth. He rocks on my lap—the right pressure and speed to have me gasping, my balls clenching and cock jerking as I spill into my boxers.

Aftershocks of pleasure have my thighs shaking as I push him backwards and wrap my lips around his nipple, teasing the tip with my tongue.

Beau yanks on my hair, his shout of pleasure loud and broken before he collapses against me. He trembles in my lap, resting against my chest with a dazed look and dark cheeks, as we both pant for breath.

"Best day ever," I mutter into Beau's hair.

Considering a doctor once told me I was cancer free, this topping that is saying a lot.

Beau laughs and presses a soft kiss to my neck. "Everything you fantasized about?"

I tighten my arms around him. "Better. So much better."

We take separate showers, which is for the best considering my anatomy is slightly different from the typical human's. The last thing I want to do after the intense make-out session with Max is scare him away because I have a little more going on behind my zipper than he might expect. Eventually, if we continue doing whatever it is we're doing, he's going to find out about my… extra appendage. Not today, though.

"Hey," Max greets from the kitchen sink, hands buried in soapy water, as I enter the kitchen while running my fingers through my still-damp hair. "Can you stay a little longer?" I grin and rest my hip on the counter beside him. He glances over. "What?"

"Do you always ask your hookups to hang around afterwards?"

His frown is fast and deep as he pulls his hands from the water and quickly dries them. As soon as his hands are free, he reaches for me and I slip easily into his arms as he backs me into the counter. The weight and warmth of his body is as close to the biblical idea of heaven as I'll ever get. "Let's get one thing clear. I don't know what's happening here, between us, but you're *not* a hookup."

I swallow and glance away. "I know."

There is something else going on between us. A connection that has endured for a decade and has nothing to do with the deal we made.

Even if I was nothing more than a quick fuck, Max isn't the type to give a hookup the heave-ho as soon as everyone has finished anyway. Knowing him, he'd offer them a glass of water and a protein bar.

"So, can you stay?" He nips at my jaw. I check the time on my wristwatch.

We met early, had coffee as well as what amounted to brunch even though it was around dinner time in Outer Banks. For us, based on the time zone, it's after lunch now. I'm not hungry and I doubt Max is either. I can stick around until at least after dinner though. Then I'll need to go home and rest so I can be ready for work tomorrow, since I have no doubt I'll be called in despite it being a scheduled day off.

"What would you like to do?" I ask as I wrap my arms around his neck. "We never explored Outer Banks. Do you want to go back?"

It'll be late but nothing in Outer Banks ever really shuts down.

Max's lips part but before he can answer, the front door slams open. "Hey, fuckface! You'd better be here."

Even after all these years I recognize that voice. Leland Mary—Max's best friend. His footsteps are loud as he stomps through the living room.

"In here," Max shouts back as we separate. Now isn't the time to let Leland catch us in an intimate embrace. I'm not sure either of us are ready for people to know we're involved.

We are involved, aren't we? If not... what exactly are we doing?

"How did your not-date—" Leland rocks to a stop. His eyes widen as he looks between the pair of us. "Fuck a duck; save a goose."

What did ducks ever do to him?

And, the things that come out of this kid's mouth. Though, Leland isn't a kid anymore. He's tall and lanky, like he'd been as a teenager, just… more now, with narrow shoulders and waist, hair short on the sides, long on top, and dyed pink. Colorful tattoos climb his arms.

Funny enough, a bag that's more duct tape than cloth hangs off his shoulder. Is it the same one from when he was a teenager? I don't doubt it is.

He's wearing a tight t-shirt that says, "*Can I pet your puppy?*" in bold font. Only it's a man in a mask, with ears on his head and a tail curling out from behind him, kneeling under the script. So… clearly not your typical puppy.

"You remember Beau." Max squeezes my shoulder as he looks down at me with a soft expression I could get used to seeing on his face.

"Are you here for his soul?" Leland comes further into the kitchen. "Because I looked it up. Contracts with minors aren't legally binding."

I blink. Wait. What?

Did he just say… *contracts with children aren't legally binding*?

"Uh… I don't think it works like that." I know for a fact it doesn't. Children can bargain away their soul the same as an adult. Human rules don't apply to creatures from the depths of so-called Hell. "But it's a moot point. Max's soul is safe."

Leland exhales, dropping onto a stool after dragging it out from under the counter. "That's good." He digs in his bag, pulls out a water bottle and sits it on the counter. "I brought holy water just in case. The banishing ritual I found online said it was the easiest thing to use when faced with a demon."

I blink.

Someone really needs to talk to Leland about his internet usage. Or just take his privileges away altogether. He found a demon summoning ritual as a teenager, and one to banish a demon as an adult. Who the hell knows what he's going to find next? Or what else he's already found.

"Where did you even get holy water?" Max snatches up the water bottle and shakes it.

Leland shrugs as he rests his forearm on the counter, apparently the picture of ease now that he knows his best friend's soul is safe. "Half of it's from the Catholic church on Newberry. The priest caught me before I finished filling the bottle and ran me off, so I had to go across town to the one near the new skate park. You know the one?" Max nods silently so I assume he does. I don't. "The priest there let me fill it up—said anyone who's trying to steal holy water probably needs it more than the Church."

What are we even supposed to say to that?

Sounds like an… adventure.

"Does holy water have any effect on you?" Max twists the cap off the bottle and sniffs. I'm pretty sure it's just water, maybe infused with some oils, but over all just water a man in a funny robe said some equally funny words over and decided to call holy.

"Not really." Not at all, but no need to disappoint Leland. He went through so much trouble to save Max's soul, after all. "God is a human concept." I take the bottle and sniff the top. "And this is just water infused with rosemary by a guy you probably shouldn't let around children."

Max and Leland snort, choking on their laughter as I turn and pour the liquid out before discarding the bottle. I sink my hands into the soapy water and start to wash the dishes, since there are several left. Silence falls and I look back to find both men watching me. "What?"

"A demon is doing your dishes, dude," Leland says with a

funny quirk to his lips, as if he's attempting not to laugh and about to fail.

"It's rude to talk about me as if I'm not here," I chastise him.

He has the decency to flush pink and rubs the back of his neck. "Sorry. This is just kind of wild. Right, Max?" My gaze shifts to Max. His face is relaxed, eyes bright, smile soft. "Max?"

He shivers. "Huh?"

"Dude. You can't get sick so what the fuck?"

Max glares. "Did you need something? Or are you here just to ruin my day?"

Leland plants his hands on his hips and widens his stance after he stands up. I press my lips together to hold back a laugh.

How many times have I seen Leland take on that same posture? In the past it usually occurred when Max was being a stubborn asshole. Doesn't look like anything has changed with them.

"Do I need a reason to visit my best friend?"

"It'd be nice if you had one when you burst into my house with a bottle of holy water to use on my demon." Max crosses his arms over his chest and lifts his chin. My heart skips a beat. Did he just say *my demon*?

"Excuse me for trying to save your eternal soul," Leland huffs as I dry my hands and turn to rest against the counter. The stubborn tilt is as familiar as Leland's stance. These two bickered for fun as teenagers and if this showdown is any indication, they still do. No wonder everyone assumed they were dating when they were teens. "And since when is he *your* demon?"

"Shut up." Max flushes pink as he glances at me before his gaze returns to Leland. "See this?" Max raises his hand and flips Leland the bird. "Sit and rotate because if I remember correctly you're the one who burst into my hospital room shouting 'let's summon a demon.' You weren't too concerned about my soul that night, were you?"

"To be fair, I didn't think you actually had a soul." Leland grins and rocks back on his heels. Anyone else would probably intervene but I've always found it entertaining how they argue. Why not sit back and enjoy the shit show?

Max's mouth drops open. "I'm insulted."

"Do you want a sticker? A gold star? Maybe a smiley face. You used to carry a packet of stickers, right Beau? He'll take one of the little emojis. An eggplant one maybe, if you've got it?"

I cover my mouth with my hand and choke down a laugh. Leland might be a nuisance but at least he's funny.

"Get out of my house." Max points towards the door.

"Maybe later." Leland turns and yanks open the fridge for a beer before crossing to the cabinet and digging inside. He clenches a bag of puff Cheetos in his hand as he leaves the kitchen. A moment later, I can hear the soft drone of the television from the living room.

"I need better friends," Max mutters as he shakes his head and meets my gaze. "Sorry about him. He's... Leland."

Yeah. That just about covers it.

"How about I head out? Give you some time with him. He probably has questions." And I should probably clean my apartment in case Max comes over anytime soon.

He sighs and reaches for me. Once more, I slide into his embrace. He rests his chin on top of my head. With anyone else, I'd push them off, and tell them to fuck off. I'm small compared to a lot of demons and it's a bit of a soft spot after all the teasing I've had to endure because of it. Max tucking me under his chin as he wraps his big arms around me might make me feel small, but not in an unpleasant way. I actually like it, being cuddled by him.

All we're missing is a bed.

We might've made it into one if Leland hadn't shown up.

Little bastard.

"I'll text, if that's okay?" Max pulls back and cups my jaw.

His mouth is soft and warm as he presses a chaste kiss to my lips. "Maybe we can get together on your next day off?"

I nod. "Yeah. I'll take you back to Outer Banks for dinner."

Max starts to grin before his brow furrows. His voice is whisper soft when he asks, "Am I allowed to tell Leland about Outer Banks?"

If I tell him no, he'll tell Leland anyway but swear him to secrecy. Maybe. But I won't ask Max to lie to either of us. Leland is his best friend. And... partly responsible for Max and I ending up here—together. Not that I'll ever tell Leland that. He'd never let us live it down.

"I'm not taking him with us on our next date," I warn because I don't care how much Leland begs or barters, no way do I want him as a third wheel.

Max's grin is wide and excited as his hands settle on my hips. "Was today a date?"

I shrug. "It wasn't a not-date."

He swoops down and captures my mouth. I quickly get lost in the taste and feel of him as he backs me into the counter. So what if Leland catches us? It'll be no less than he deserves for busting uninvited into Max's house.

CHAPTER
EIGHT
MAXTON

Who needs enemies with a lifelong best friend like Leland Mary?

He's sitting sans pants on my sofa, the bag of Cheetos he stole from my cabinet between his spread thighs and a pilfered beer in hand, without a single care in the world. Orange dust stains his pointed chin and fingers. If I thought he wouldn't kick me back, I'd plant my foot somewhere sensitive.

"You're an asshole," I say as I fall beside him on the sofa with my own beer and yank the Cheetos away from him. The last thing I want a handful of is his cock. I don't need to be disappointed any more today.

"What did I do?" Leland licks his index finger before reaching into the chip bag again. I don't bother telling him how gross it is that he's about to put his damp fingers into my Cheetos. It won't be the first time, after all. Or the last. At this point, if we don't have each other's germs already, we never will.

"Holy water. Really?" I shake my head and tip the beer back, swallowing half the contents before diving into the Cheetos bag.

Leland shrugs. "You're my best friend. What did you expect me to do?"

A smile is playing at the edge of his mouth. It might be worth it to punch him—just once. Instead, I sigh because shit, can I really be mad at him? Even if he was just fucking around when he showed up, I also know he got the water as a last-ditch effort to help me fend off a demon, if I needed it. His help isn't necessary. Beau is… He's wonderful.

It's insane how much I like him. How much I've always liked him. How can I not though? There's something magnetic about the demon. Everything about him draws me in, even the demon face he'd been so reluctant to show me. If not for Leland's untimely arrival, he would still be here. Maybe I could've convinced him to remove his glamor again.

Would he have finally told me why he doesn't collect the souls of sick children, even though it will end their suffering and prolong their life? Or would we have found a better use for our mouths? I'll never know now.

Best friends. Hate to love 'em.

"I told you before, if you're going to fantasize about the hot night nurse, at least let me leave first. I love you, but not like that," Leland says around a mouthful.

"Shut up. Why are we friends again?"

Leland throws his bare thigh over my leg and dips his hand into the Cheetos bag as he relaxes back against the arm of the sofa. "All your other friends fucked off when you got cancer so it's me or no one."

He's not wrong. As an adult, I struggle to make and keep friends. I'm either too serious or not serious enough. Before I got sick, we had a wide social circle. Both of us played for the basketball team in high school—me as a point guard and Leland as a power forward—so more often than not, we spent time with our teammates. On and off the court.

I thought of them as my friends. How could I not after days spent at the pool or arcade, nights chilling at one another's houses? Then I got sick and slowly, they disappeared. Only Leland stuck around, going so far as to temporarily move with my family from New York to Memphis, Tennessee while I got treatment, with his parents' full support, so he could be with me whenever possible.

Those first long, difficult afternoons were spent listening to music, watching movies, or playing board games with missing pieces while he tried to keep my spirits up. Eventually, out of desperation, we took to reading anything we could get our hands on. Mostly manga.

More often than not, when I had a hard day and couldn't stay awake for any length of time, I'd wake up to find Leland stretched out at the foot of my bed, nose buried in some book, snacking on my lunch because we both knew I wasn't going to eat it. And if I did, I was only going to vomit.

A thank you for all the time and opportunities he sacrificed to be with me was never necessary because Leland *knows*. He's well aware of how much I love and appreciate him to this day. He's so much more than my best friend. A brother I never had.

If the day ever comes and he's the one lying sick in a hospital bed, I'll be the first to draw a shitty summoning circle in cheap chalk and hope his hot night nurse has strange eyes and a forked tongue.

"Until death do us part." I hold my bottle out.

Leland taps the neck of his against mine. "So, I assume since you brought your demon home, the not-date went well."

"It was a date." I flip him and his smug smile off. He can shut right the fuck up. So what if I'd arrived thinking it was just a meeting between former acquaintances. It had started that way but after the question and answer portion of our meeting was done, when we decided to get lunch together, it became so much more. I smile to myself.

"And?" Leland prompts, flicking his tongue against his index finger before sucking the digit between his lips. I ignore his behavior. He's doing it to annoy me. Today, it won't work. Too much good shit happened for me to get upset over Leland being himself.

"He took me to this place called Outer Banks. Oh!" I dig in my pocket for my phone. "Did you know the mystery of the Bermuda Triangle has been solved?"

Leland's eyes widen as I open my internet browser. "Since when?"

"I'm looking." I tap and find an article on what appears to be a reputable website. Leland reads over my shoulder, scanning the short passage from National Ocean Services.

"Wait. So… their reasoning is nature and human *stupidity*." Leland sits back and finishes his beer. We sit in silence, absorbing the news that the mystery is weather and dumbassery. "Yeah. I guess that makes the most sense. People struggle to drive and we have road signs. The open ocean or endless sky—not surprised." He shrugs, stands up, and slips into the kitchen, returning with two cold beers. "I'm a little disappointed it's not magic or aliens."

"Same." I accept the beer as Leland falls at my side again. "Aliens would be more fun."

He arches an eyebrow as we open our beers. "What need do you have for aliens when you're dating a demon?"

"Who says the alien is for me? I've seen your browsing history."

Tentacles. A lot of tentacles.

I'm not judging. How can I judge him considering who I just made out with? And will make out with again, if Beau is willing the next time I see him.

"Are you going to tell me about your date or not?" Leland snatches the Cheetos bag back. I don't fight him for it, not after watching him give his finger a blow job.

I take a long pull from my beer, the crisp taste bursting over my tongue like a slightly bitter apple, and settle into the sofa. Leland eats the Cheetos as I tell him about Outer Banks, the people I saw, the places we visited.

There's so much to explain and I'm sure I leave a lot out, but Leland listens as I talk, and talk, and talk, voice growing in volume and pitch.

When it comes time to tell Leland how Beau looks without his glamor, I pause. Beau was hesitant to show me, and even though he said it's okay to tell Leland about Outer Banks, I didn't ask about his demon form. It seems more... personal, like something Beau should show Leland himself, if he ever wants to.

"What?" Leland asks when the silence has stretched too long. "Tell me."

"Beau showed me what he looks like when he doesn't look human," I finally confess.

Leland sits up and turns, crowding me against the arm of the sofa. "Was he scary? Hot?" He sounds like an overexcited teenager asking for gossip about their crush. His face is so close to mine our noses are almost touching. I can smell the cheese on his breath. It's a little gross. "Did he have horns? Fangs? Extra appendages?"

I shove him and he topples backwards. "All I'm saying is I thought he was hot. If you want to know what he looks like, you'll have to ask him, but"—I point a stern finger—"don't be fucking annoying. He was shy about showing me."

The last thing I want is my best friend to run Beau off by asking one too many times to see his demon form.

Leland huffs and reaches for his beer. "Fine. Can I at least come see Outer Banks? Maybe a hot werewolf will pound me against a tree."

I blink and stare at him. He owns and operates a non-profit animal shelter. Should I be concerned that he wants a werewolf to pound him against a tree? Is that... It's not bestiality, right? I mean, a werewolf is part man. Surely Leland doesn't want said werewolf to fuck him as a wolf. Maybe he does. And, really, maybe I don't want to know. What Leland does in his free time, with or without a werewolf, isn't my concern. More power to him either way, I suppose.

"Maybe. Eventually. Just… can you be chill for once in your life about this? I really like Beau."

I want to see where our relationship goes and it won't go anywhere fast if Leland chases Beau away.

Leland seems to think about my request before he blows out a breath. "Shit. I'm sorry. I was worried when you didn't answer your phone though. Did you guys have more plans today?"

I shrug this time. "Not really? Maybe dinner."

Possibly more kissing. If the kiss Beau gave me before he left is any indication, there would've been a lot more kissing. Or more. I'm so down with more. It's been a while since I got laid— since my last boyfriend and I broke up over a year ago. Unlike Leland, I'm not down to go to pound town with anyone who shoots me a smile and buys me a drink.

Leland leans forward and picks up his phone. "It's not too late to invite him back."

"What? No way. I just sent him home."

The idea has its appeal but do I really want to look that desperate for Beau's time and attention? Plus, what if he has work tomorrow? By now, he's probably home, showered and undressed. I'm not asking him to get up and pull clothes on just so we can have dinner tonight instead of on his next day off.

"Don't be a chicken shit," Leland says as he stands up. "Tell him I left and ask him, I don't know—if he wants to get an early dinner. Demons have to eat too, right?"

Do they? I honestly don't know. Beau ate lunch but was it out of necessity?

"What part of 'I just sent him home' are you not hearing?"

Leland yanks on his clothes after sucking his fingers clean, all while rolling his eyes. "At least text him. Alright? You like him, so don't be a dumbass and not shoot him a follow-up text. Promise me."

"Yeah. Okay." A follow-up text I can do. But dragging Beau back to my place, or even somewhere out to dinner tonight? No. We can have dinner next time he's free, like we agreed. I'm not that impatient. At least, I don't want to appear as if I am.

Leland pats me on the head. "Good boy."

I swat his hand and shove him away.

Fucker.

CHAPTER NINE

T he long work week is filled with endless examples of human stupidity.

A man climbing a ladder fell fifteen feet and broke several bones, one of which required surgery to repair, much to his wife's displeasure. I'm pretty sure she would've rather him simply die. I can't say I blame her, not after listening to the way he spoke to her the entire time she quietly sat at his side. If I was her, I would've given the ladder a little shake and waited to call EMS as long as possible, *if at all*.

A teenager with a non-life-threatening self-inflicted gunshot wound because he decided to play with his parents' gun. Said parents had to be escorted from the emergency room after they started a screaming match in the hallway over who was to blame. Both of them are at fault, as far I'm concerned. Who leaves a loaded firearm unsecured in a house with curious kids?

Some people shouldn't have children. Or be married, for that matter.

A woman who attempted to pierce her own nipples with a hot needle several days ago learned the hard way you need more than a sharp object when poking holes in your body. And heat isn't the secret ingredient when it comes to body piercing. Sterile equipment is always a good place to start, not fire. Training doesn't hurt either. In fact, there's a good reason both are recommended.

Humanity. How they've lasted this long is the real mystery. I mean, seriously. Most of the injuries I treat every day can be avoided with a little common sense. And I do mean a little.

The next idiot who wanders into the emergency department will be someone else's problem. For the next two days, until I'm back for my three twelve-hour, regularly scheduled days, I plan to ignore my phone completely. I have no doubt my boss will call me tomorrow morning in a solid attempt to get me to pull more overtime but when I don't answer, she'll have to find someone else.

If I don't get some real time outside of the ED I'm going to turn in my resignation. I can't keep doing this—working twelve-hour shifts, five days a week, which is two more than I'm supposed to work. Everyone needs a break, human or not.

Just as I shut my locker after withdrawing my bag, my phone vibrates in my pocket. When I pull it free and see Maxton's name, I smile.

We've been texting on and off since the day I took him to Outer Banks for brunch. And kissed him afterwards. Tomorrow, after I get some much-needed rest, I'm supposed to take him back there to explore.

MAXTON

Do I need to stage a rescue?

BEAU

Not this time. I'm about to escape.

MAXTON

Perfect.

I slip my phone in my pocket, shoulder my bag and make a beeline for the door, still dressed in my scrubs. Even when I hear one of my coworkers call my name, I don't stop, just wave over my shoulder. "See you next week."

The weekend is their problem. I won't be coming in or swapping shifts with anyone because they have a birthday party, baby shower, wedding or some other family event that they only *just* learned about, and thus didn't have time to request time off to attend. I've sacrificed my free time for them too many times, but not anymore.

I want to spend some time with Maxton—not just sightseeing, but kissing too. Maybe more, if he's up for it.

He's been understanding about my hectic schedule so far, but how long can I keep him on the back burner before he simply gets tired of me waiting to make him a priority?

Pushing open the employee exit, I stumble to a stop.

"Max. What are you doing here?"

He looks away and rubs the back of his neck as a bright flush climbs his cheeks. "I was going to pretend to have a heart attack if you didn't show up in the next hour."

My laugh is abrupt as I approach him. "Really?" A heart attack. Just so he could, what—see me? "You might've got a completely different nurse. Then what?"

He clears his throat. "I uh… I was going to say my boyfriend worked in the ER, and I was *really scared*. Maybe cry."

I blink. That… That does not sound like something Max would do. His best friend, however—"How long did it take Leland to come up with that plan?"

Max looks down at his phone, thumbing the screen so it lights up and unlocks. "About two minutes."

"You would've been trapped in the ER for hours," I say as we move further from the exit. With shift change people are flowing in and out of the building; I don't want to be in the way of anyone in a rush.

"Nah." He shakes his head and shoves his hands into his pockets. "I would've left AMA"—*against medical advice*—"and my concerned boyfriend would've insisted on taking me home to monitor me since I was being an idiot."

It might've worked too. My boss would've most likely told me to look after Maxton at home and bring him back if necessary, since I was already working overtime. I don't know if I should be impressed or horrified at his and Leland's well thought out deception. One they came up within the span of two minutes, apparently.

"Now what?" I ask.

He's here. I'm off work. What next?

"Oh. Um." Maxton sinks his teeth into his bottom lip, for the first time looking unsure of himself. "Can I walk you home? I know you're probably tired, and I don't want to keep you out, but…"

His gaze drops and he trails off, but I have a feeling I know what he isn't saying. He wanted to see me, if only for the time it takes him to walk me home. It's… sweet, but I don't usually walk home.

Most of the time I slip into the metro bathroom and pop into my living room when I'm sure everyone who saw me enter is gone. I don't actually live anywhere near the hospital—or in the city, for that matter. If we attempt to walk, we'd never make it.

"Have you had breakfast?" I ask.

Maxton frowns. It's honestly kind of adorable how confused he looks. "What?"

It's just after six in the morning. The city is just waking up around us. Maxton has probably been standing out here for an hour, waiting for me to emerge—or not, so he can fake a heart attack—so I doubt he's actually had breakfast. Did he even get a cup of coffee to enjoy while he waited?

"There's a cafe not far. We could grab a bite to eat—some coffee?" Even though I just came off a twelve-hour shift and could easily go to sleep, I won't suffer if I don't. Sleep isn't a necessity, just something I enjoy the hell out of. Like food. And sex.

"Breakfast sounds good," Maxton says.

Even though he's doing a good job hiding it, I can tell he's excited to be grabbing something as simple as food together after our week apart. The fact he seems to have actually missed me has me stepping forward and pressing a soft kiss to the corner of his mouth.

When I pull back, Maxton blinks several times before grinning. "Hi."

I laugh. "Hello."

He groans and rubs the back of his neck. "I'm so awkward."

"It's cute," I assure him. "I like it."

I like him. Is that any surprise?

Max huffs. "I feel like I'm sixteen again with a crush on my hot night nurse."

"Bright side," I say as I take his hand and pull him further away from the employee exit, in the direction of the cafe, "I don't have to pretend not to notice the awkward boner as I help you wash up."

By the end of our time together I'd become a pro at pretending not to notice Max's reaction as I helped him, as he did his best to pretend like it wasn't happening. He'd been a child as far as I was concerned, with the desires of an adult, unable to take care of his basic hygiene. I did my best to make it as quick and professional as possible. How he took care of himself and his body's needs after I helped him clean up and dress was his business. I didn't want to know; I still don't even now.

"Oh god," Maxton whispers, his voice cracking as his hand tightens around mine. "Just kill me. Now, please."

I'm being awful, teasing him, but he makes it so easy, and he doesn't seem to really mind. Still, in the spirit of cutting him a break—"How was your week?"

"Not bad, actually." He laces our fingers together so we're

holding hands and I'm not just pulling him along. "It was a slow week at the shop. My little brother just got his ASE so Mom's planning a dinner to celebrate."

"Your dad owns a mechanic shop, right?"

The ASE is the certification all mechanics need in order to work.

Maxton glances at me. "You remember?"

Yeah, I remember. The nights when he was tired but couldn't sleep because he was in pain, or nauseous, or just homesick, I took the time to sit and talk until he was ready to try to sleep without being medicated.

He hated the melatonin we gave the kids on the floor because it made him groggy when he woke up. Plus, he had nightmares sometimes because of the medication and I didn't want him to suffer more than he was already. Bad sleep can sometimes be worse than no sleep for a sick kid.

"You were going to get your ASE after high school too, right?" As a teenager, he'd been excited about working with his dad one day. Did he change his mind? Pick another career path? It seems unlikely.

He nods. "Yeah. Because I missed so much school and I was so far behind, I got my GED and took my ASE early after we came back to New York. I've been working with Dad since I was seventeen."

We turn a corner and I see the cafe just down the street. Neither of us are in a rush. I'm happy to hold Maxton's hand and take our time.

"I'm proud of you." He had a goal and never lost sight of it, even when no one would have thought badly of him for reevaluating his life after such a close encounter with death. "I bet your dad was pretty excited when you started working with him."

Maxton chuckles; the sound is soft and warm. "He was. Worried too." He pauses and I glance up. "Even though the cancer was gone, I was still underweight—weak—and everyone was scared it would come back even though I tried to assure them I was okay. Dad mostly had me shuffling paperwork and taking phone calls. Eventually I told him if he wasn't going to let me use my ASE, I'd find a shop that would. He eased up some, after that."

"You being sick was hard on everyone but I'm glad you stood up for yourself." I stop outside the cafe and pull the door open.

Maxton grasps it and I slip under his arm with a grateful smile.

The cafe is crowded but near the back, stuffed into a corner, is an empty table. I make a beeline for it with Maxton on my heels. Before I can pull out my chair, Maxton is there, doing it for me.

CHAPTER
TEN

MAXTON

After breakfast—a coffee for both of us, a sticky-sweet cinnamon roll for Beau and a BLT with a fried egg for me—we join the early morning foot traffic as they rush towards their final destination.

I'm not sure how far Beau lives from the hospital but I'm determined to walk him home, even if that means spending more time on the metro than I normally do.

"In here." He pushes the bathroom door open and waves me through.

An older man washing his hands at the sink briefly glances up before minding his own business. A couple of the stalls are occupied. Beau steps up to the sink to wash his hands, but as soon as the old man finishes, he grasps my hand and pulls me into one of the stalls. As I open my mouth to ask what we're doing he slaps his hand over it and shakes his head. I'm not opposed to sex in a metro bathroom but maybe it's something we should talk about first?

Beau doesn't seem keyed up as his thumb brushes back and forth through the scruff on my jaw. Instead, we stand in silence for several minutes, listening as the bathroom empties out.

Once we're alone, Beau lowers his hand to my shoulder and

leans in as I lay my hands on his hips. His breath is hot on my ear when he whispers, "I don't live nearby so I usually… come and go in my own unique way."

"Oh." He gets home the same way he got us to Outer Banks. Being able to disappear and reappear at will makes his commute to and from work a lot shorter than the average person, I'm sure, but since I'm as human as humans can be and can't travel the way he does…

Disappointment settles like a boulder on my shoulders.

"I guess—"

"Do you—"

We both pause before I say, "You first."

"Do you want to come over?"

Do I want to… What kind of question is that?

"Yes." My voice is too loud in the otherwise silent bathroom, echoing off the tile. I wince before lowering my voice. "I mean… if you're not tired?"

He did just pull a twelve-hour shift. If last night was anything like some of his other nights, he probably wants to go home and pass the fuck out. The last thing I want to do is keep him up when he needs rest.

Beau shakes his head. "I, uh, don't really need as much sleep as your average person."

I open my mouth to ask exactly how much sleep he needs but the bathroom door opens. Beau steps forward and wraps his arm around my back, lifting his eyebrow in silent question. I nod and feel the same sharp tug under my ribcage as last time we traveled together. It's only a second before my feet are on solid ground again, and this time I'm not as disoriented. Beau keeps his arm around me until my knees stop knocking together, then releases me.

He glances around and I follow his gaze. "So uh… this is me —home, sweet home."

It's well decorated, bigger than my place—and cleaner than

when I invited him over—but pretty typical for a mid-range income in the city.

"It's nice."

"Feel free to look around."

I step away—it's only fair I investigate his bookshelf, after all —but pause as my gaze sweeps over a set of floor-to-ceiling windows for a second time.

Nowhere in the city has that kind of view.

Trees stretch out for miles, butting up against the side of a towering snow-capped mountain. A flock of birds soars above the pines, screeching in a language only they know. There's a peaceful hum that is almost impossible to find in the city. And something else I can't define in the air. It settles over me like a warm, comfortable blanket.

Magic, maybe.

I glance at Beau. He's at the stove, putting on a kettle and humming under his breath. The sunlight streaming through the windows illuminates his blonde hair, giving him a halo when I know for a fact he has horns.

"Are we in Outer Banks?"

Where else could we be?

Beau smiles over his shoulder, hair falling into his bright eyes. "Is that okay? I did promise to bring you back to explore…"

I'm not mad about the impromptu visit. My brother is helping my dad at the shop today and I have nothing planned with Leland. After not seeing Beau for almost a week, spending some time with him is exactly what I want. We don't necessarily have to explore Outer Banks either. If he wants to rest I'll be just as happy hanging out on the sofa.

What we do on the sofa is entirely up to him but I'm not against doing more of what we did on my sofa back in the city.

"Have you lived here long?" I ask as I move away from the breathtaking view out his windows and into his kitchen. I can explore his bookcase later.

"A while now. Anywhere else and I have to provide identification, work history, references, so on and so forth. I can but…" He shrugs as he turns away from the kettle and rests his hip on the counter. I tuck my hands into my pockets and mirror his position. Only a foot of space separates us. My hands itch with the desire to pull him close. "I can stay in one city longer if I don't leave too much of a paper trail."

"How long have you been in New York?" I ask around a sudden lump in my throat. How long does he usually stay in one place? Will I wake up one day to find him gone again? Vanished into thin air?

"I came to the city after Memphis." He turns away, taking the whistling kettle off the stove. "New last name. New papers." He fills two mugs with water and adds tea bags. "It'll be a while before I need to move on again. It's only when the people around you start to get old they notice you're not aging with them."

"Beau…" I cup the back of his elbow and pull him away from the counter.

It sounds as if he's moved around *a lot*. How many people has he left behind? People he cared for who started to age and ask questions he couldn't answer. Is the whole of his existence a series of goodbyes?

How can he stand it?

"It's okay." He lays his hand on my chest, a soft smile pulling at his mouth but not reaching his eyes. "Just the nature of my life."

I slide my hand up the back of his arm before cupping his neck and tugging him forward. "Promise you won't move on without telling me." I may be human—doomed to grow old like all the others—but I know his secret and I can take it to the grave with me. We don't ever have to say goodbye, not for a number of years. My lips twitch. "And say something nice at my funeral. But don't let Leland say shit. God knows what secrets he'll share once I'm dead and gone."

Beau huffs and slaps my chest. "Not funny."

"It's a little funny," I argue. His lips twitch but he shakes his head. I brush my mouth over his, softly at first, but harder when he leans in with a soft sigh and parts his lips. I tug him against my chest and he grasps my sides, melting against me with a quiet hum. My stomach clenches and my cock starts to harden behind my zipper as I slip my tongue into his mouth before pulling back.

Beau blinks, a furrow developing between his brows. "What?"

"Is it weird that I like kissing you when you're not using a glamor?"

Right now, he looks human. No one passing him on the street would know he's so much more than that. But I know. It's one of my favorite things about him.

Like before, his eyes change first. Then the rest of him, until everything that makes him human is gone. I cup his jaw and drag my thumb over his mouth. His lips part and his tongue flicks out against the tip. My hand tingles and I suck in a sharp breath before slotting my mouth over his again.

His hands are everywhere—my chest and stomach, sides and back—as his forked tongue curls around mine. Heat builds at the base of my spine as I get lost in the taste and feel of him. Even as a demon, he's smaller than me—compact but muscular. I love the way he fits in my arms. I hold him against my chest before slipping my hands beneath his shirt.

Beau makes this sound deep in the back of his throat and I swallow it as he leans into my touch, dropping his hands to my ass before he rolls our hips together. My cock is hard, leaking into my boxers, and if the bulge pressing against mine is any indication, he's just as hard.

I run my hands down his sides, exploring the spiderweb veins as I go, and slide my hands into the front of his dark green scrubs. He gasps, yanking his mouth away from mine, back arching as I close my fist around him, eyes going wide as I come to a complete stop.

Beau pants for breath as I stare down at him. He…

A handful of dick doesn't even begin to explain what I'm holding because if I'm not mistaken… Beau has two. Two dicks.

Like an exploding star, possibilities burst in my mind's eye. All the ways. What I can do to him. What he can do to me.

He steps back and I follow, tightening my palm. I press him against the counter, his cocks encased tightly together in my fist. My fingers don't touch as I stroke from root to leaking tips.

"Maxton." His voice is weak and shaky.

"Something you forgot to mention, Beau?" I tease even as I pull back just enough to look down and see my hand disappearing into his scrubs. The elastic is pulled away from his abdomen but I can't see what I'm touching. It's damn obvious though as I stroke my thumb over his damp slits.

"I—" His voice cracks and he clears his throat. "I was going to tell you. Eventually."

"It's hot." I press a kiss to the corner of his mouth as I start to pump his cocks—slowly at first, then faster when he begins to pant for breath. "Think of all the fun we can have."

Shit. I'm having fun now, exploring him with my fingers, learning the shape of his pair of cocks, watching him fall apart in my hand. I slip my other hand into his scrubs and take one in each, pumping them in sync.

My knuckles bump together on each stroke and Beau's hands curl around my shoulders as he thrusts into my fists. He's leaking so much each stroke is smooth and easy.

"Maxton." Beau's breath is hot on my collarbone. He drops his hand and yanks on the button to undo my jeans, pulling my zipper down and shoving his hands into the fabric. I grunt and rock into his warm hand as soon as his fingers close around my dripping cock.

I know how sharp and dangerous his nails are and it sends a secret thrill down my spine that this demon is touching me so carefully. My balls pull tight against my body and I'm harder than I've ever been as our mouths meet in a clash of lips, tongues and teeth.

Beau supports most of our weight as he leans against the counter and works my cock as I work both of his. One is slightly smaller than the other, but even small isn't an accurate description because it's a solid six or seven inches—just… average. The other, however, is maybe eight or nine and much thicker. My hole clenches and I stutter out a breath.

What would it be like to have one of his cocks inside me while I jack both of us off? Or, shit—both his cocks inside of me at the same time. I've never had an interest in double penetration before but now…

The breath shudders out of my lungs as my balls throb and my cock pulses. Wet heat spreads in my boxers as Beau tightens his fist. Pleasure rocks down my spine. Beau moans and pulls his mouth from mine, burying his face in my neck as his cocks jerk in my hands. I jack him through his orgasm as mine continues to roll over me in waves, loosening my muscles and making my knees weak.

"Shit," Beau whispers, pressing a soft kiss to my throat. "I needed that."

I chuckle and press my forehead against his temple. "Me too."

CHAPTER
ELEVEN

BEAU

We stumble towards the bathroom, my knees still knocking together as I push the door open and slip inside with Max right behind me. I turn on the shower, letting it warm before I turn to Max.

His face is flushed, his expression soft as he yanks his shirt over his head and discards it. The sight of him is a pleasure but not enough to distract me from the sudden ache in my stomach. He and I look nothing alike—not when I'm without my glamor.

I hesitate before pulling my shirt off and dropping it in a pile with his. Max's heated gaze never leaves me as we undress; his eyes track every movement I make. He wets his swollen bottom lip with his tongue. I pause before shoving my scrubs down my hips, letting them pool around my ankles before kicking them away.

After the expert hand jobs Max gave me in the kitchen—and the nervous twist in my stomach about how he'll handle actually seeing me, all of me—I'm soft. My cocks rest against my thighs, lying together as always. If Max is interested in another round it won't take much to get me excited again. And... I exhale. If the light in his eyes is any indication, he's game for a second round.

I step through the sliding glass doors into the shower; Max

follows, crowding me into a corner. The tile is cold against my back. The warm water beats down around us, slicking our skin and fogging the shower door. His gaze is heavy on my face before it drops to my cocks.

My chest rocks as I pant for breath, fist my hands at my sides, and let him look his fill. He already knows I'm different—*a demon* —so there's no use hiding from him. I don't want to hide, not really. If who I really am is too much for him, it's better that we find out sooner rather than later.

An—if I'm not mistaken—aroused flush spreads across Max's scruffy cheeks and down his neck. He ghosts his fingers over my tapered cockhead, teasing the slit until I plump under his soft touch.

"Max?" The question in my voice is unmistakable.

What is he thinking? What is he planning?

The silence is killing me. I need him to say something. *Anything.*

"You're amazing. Beautiful," Max rasps before slotting his mouth over mine. Our tongues meet and slide together. He tastes fresh and clean, but also slightly bitter from the coffee we had. I moan as I wrap my fingers around his cock. He groans against my mouth and takes my cocks in a single fist as we work together, chasing mutual bliss.

Everything about his touch is perfect—the pressure and speed, the little twist he adds on the upstroke. How he teases the sensitive underside of one cock with his thumb before giving the same attention to the other one. No part of me is neglected. Pleasure pools liquid hot, like that first sip of hot chocolate on a cold day, in my stomach as my thighs tense and I roll my hips.

I just came and still, I won't last.

My belly quivers as I pant into his mouth. We aren't even kissing now, just sharing oxygen as we rock against one another until Max releases my cocks to bat my hand away from his. I gape at him, disappointed to be denied my release when I was already so close, but he steps forward, slides his cock between mine, and closes both his hands around us.

"Oh fuck," I rasp, laying my hands over top before fucking my cocks alongside his. He's hot and slick, hard as steel, and leaking all over my shafts. His hands are just the right amount of rough. I rush headlong and recklessly closer and closer to the edge until I'm standing on my tiptoes, staring into his eyes, heaving for every breath I take. "Max. I—Shit."

I squeeze my eyes shut. A shiver works its way down my spine as I shoot, making a mess of Max's hands, cock and balls. My thighs burn as I fall back against the wall with a shaky breath.

"Holy shit." Max follows. His hands tighten around us as his cum soaks the base of my cocks. I can feel the pulse of his cock, the heat of his cum, and it only makes me hungry for more of him. I tighten my hands around his, making him squeeze tighter but stroke slower as we quiver and pant through the aftershocks before falling apart, collapsing against the tile.

Max leans against the opposite wall, his chest heaving as his bright eyes meet mine. He clears his throat but when he speaks, his voice is still raw. "Was that as good as I think it was?"

Over the course of my long life, I've had a lot of sex both as a human and as a demon. But a simple hand job in the shower with Max blew all of my past encounters out of the water.

I swallow several times and push away from the wall. "On a scale of one to ten—at least a twelve."

Max's smile is blinding as he joins me in the middle of the shower. I reach for the shampoo. "Do you wash your legs?"

Max's brow furrows. "What?"

"You know…" I motion as if I'm washing my legs and feet with my free hand. "Do you—"

"What kind of question is that? Who isn't washing their lower body? Do *you* wash *your* legs?" Max sounds flummoxed, as if the idea of someone not washing their legs is unbelievable.

"Yeah." I shrug as I squeeze shampoo into his hand then

mine. "But some people don't. They say gravity and soap washes them."

I set the shampoo down and start to lather my hair.

"What? No. Who are these people?" Max pushes his fingers into his hair, pulling at the strands as he looks down at me.

"Just humans." It's a whole debate people have with their family, friends, co-workers. Now anytime I shower, I'm reminded of someone asking me if I wash my legs when I shower. I feel obligated to pass the trauma on to as many unsuspecting victims as I can.

"The wrong kind of humans," Max mutters, bowing under the water to rinse his hair before standing upright. "I mean, I get it if you physically can't do it because of a mobility issue. Or if you're struggling in some other way, like, with depression, or another illness that makes even bothering to get in the shower a chore, but otherwise... what the fuck? Wash your legs."

I laugh, and happen to silently agree, as we continue to share hot water and soft touches, the silence comfortable and easy. We wash off under the spray—lower bodies included—get out when we're done, and dry off.

I give Max a pair of worn sweats that mold to his ass like they were made for him. The way they cup his thighs has my mouth watering before I escape to throw his jeans in the wash. He comes out of my bedroom just as I exit the laundry closet.

"Ready?" I ask, slipping my feet into a pair of shoes after my glamor settles into place.

Max hums and looks up from tying his laces. "What did you have in mind?"

I take his hand and tug him forward. He comes easily, wrapping his arms around my shoulders before I teleport us from my apartment to the heart of Outer Banks. The park is teeming with people—humans and parahumans alike. Some are just enjoying the warmth of the day, courtesy of magic and the ley line Outer Banks sits on, while others are absorbed in fun with family or friends.

I slip my hand into Maxton's as he looks around, a little wide eyed but smiling nonetheless, dark hair swaying in the breeze, and pull him towards one of the many paths that lead out of the park.

He falls into step with me. "What's the time difference between here and New York?"

"Five hours ahead."

It's barely mid-morning in New York; it's after lunch here.

The Atlantic Ocean sits between us and the city. What used to take humans months to cross, and hours still now by plane, is a thought away for me and anyone else who shares similar talents.

His gaze swings to me, lips parting as he takes a deep breath. "We're somewhere in the UK—near Ben Nevis."

From the windows in my apartment, he had a clear view of it.

"The... UK." He swallows.

Has he ever traveled outside of America? Is this his first time on foreign soil? Does Outer Banks even count, considering the parahuman city has no ties to any human government? They don't even know we exist. Outer Banks isn't somewhere just anyone can travel to get a stamp on their passport.

"Scotland to be exact. The western edge of the Grampian Mountains."

His mouth tips up at the corner. "I uh... I can find Scotland on a map but otherwise..." Max shrugs and I squeeze his hand. "I'll look it up when I get home."

Would he prefer I take him home, now that he knows just how far away from New York we are? I don't want to cut our time together short but if he wants to go, I won't make him stay. "Do you still want to explore?"

His hand tightens around mine. "Show me. I want to see your home."

I grin and drag him onwards, towards the shopping center.

The first shop that catches his eye is another occult shop. Unlike The Bone Tarot, it's run by a grumpy old man who silently glares at us from behind the counter as we step inside. It's filled with floor-to-ceiling bookshelves.

No magic crystals or potions here. Just another kind of magic.

Shelves of knowledge, about all things supernatural. Here, Max could learn the answer to damn near any question he has. But even if he enjoys reading, he prefers asking me about the community I'm part of. This past week he texted me half a dozen questions about Outer Banks and the people who call it home. Some of them, I suspect, were asked on behalf of Leland.

"This place is amazing," Max whispers as he walks the aisles, stopping to inspect any book that catches his eye. I follow along, smiling as I watch him flip through pages, reading a passage here and there.

I feel a little drunk on his presence, his joy as he shows me a passage about Everlost—another supernatural city. "Can we visit one day, you think?"

I swallow and nod. *One day.* Because Max is thinking long term too.

This thing between us is growing fast and I have no desire or intention to slow us down, much less stop. Max means something to me.

I'm pretty sure I'm half in love with him. If not already all the way there.

It's too fast, makes zero sense, but… it's the truth.

I'm in love with Maxton Grant.

"Yeah. You'll love it there," I say around the sudden lump in my throat. Max grins. "If you want the book, the grump at the desk will let you check it out for three days. Or I can buy it for you?"

His smile is soft and sweet as he shakes his head. "Maybe

some other time? Not sure I want to be carrying a ton of books around. Plus, Leland will just steal any book I take home."

I laugh under my breath. He would.

"We can bring him next time," I offer.

"Yeah?" He snags my hand and pulls me close.

"If you want." I don't mind Leland tagging along from time to time. If he gets too annoying I can feed him to the wolves —literally.

Max bows his head and brushes his mouth against mine. "Thank you, Beau."

"You don't have to thank me for anything."

All of this, being with him, is a pleasure.

He pecks me on the mouth again and we continue to wander through the shop before hitting the streets once more.

Every time we step into another shop, Max finds something else to ask questions about. I love every second of it—spending this day with him, showing him my home.

It's well after noon in New York, and closer to dinner time in Scotland, when I hear his stomach grumble. "Hungry? Do you want to eat at I Know a Guy or try something new?"

He seems to think about it for a minute as we step out of the way of the flow of traffic. "Something new?"

"There's a place down here I think you'll like," I say.

Just as we round the corner, a dozen or so steps away from For Fox Sake—a bistro run by a family of fox shifters—an all too familiar voice shouts, "Beau!"

I stumble to a stop. Running isn't an option. Fuck knows I've tried in the past but… Ambrose is the kind of persistent bastard who would chase me down like a dedicated hellhound. Or best friend. Which, he sort of is. Only, I'm still more than sort of pissed at him.

I groan and turn to face the demon as he crosses the street. His sharp gaze flickers between Max and me, a feral grin pulling at his mouth, exposing a sharp fang. Why he doesn't use a glamor to appear less like a creature of the night isn't a topic of conversation I want to ever engage in with him. Some conversations aren't worth having.

"Ambrose. It's been a while."

"You've been avoiding me," he says. I have. There's no point denying it. If he hadn't called out to me I would've continued to ignore him.

"This is Maxton—Max. And this is Ambrose. An old friend of mine."

Max thrusts his free hand out, a polite smile in place. "Nice to meet you."

Ambrose looks at his hand long and hard before taking it and jerking Max forward. A growl vibrates the back of my throat as Ambrose inhales deeply, an interested gleam illuminating his eyes. "Nice."

I grasp the back of Max's shirt and tug him backward. "Hands off."

Max isn't a soul to be collected—not by me, him, or anyone else for that matter. He will live and die after a long, healthy, human life, before being reborn once more.

Ambrose holds his hands up and takes a step back. "I'm not interested in him. Fuck knows you could do with a soul like his after your last debacle." Ambrose rolls his eyes and just keeps right on talking. "What kind of demon accepts a favor in exchange for *anything?*" He tsks and shakes his head. I won't miss him if I send him back from whence he came, by-default best friend or not. "Don't look at me like that. You know it's true. It's been what? Ten years—"

"Did you need something?" I snap. I refuse to look at Max. I can feel his gaze like a hot poker on the side of my face. He knows Ambrose is talking about him, and the deal we made.

Ambrose huffs and shoves his hands into his pockets. "When did you turn into such a moody bastard?"

Does he really need to ask? Because the answer should be obvious.

Right around the last time I saw him a year or more ago and he decided to give me unsolicited advice on my ill-advised choices. He clearly hasn't learned when to keep his mouth shut since then. By now, he should know. If I wanted his opinion—*any* demon's opinion about my choices, for that matter—I would fucking ask for it.

TWELVE
MAXTON

Maybe no one will ever mistake me for a genius but I'm not an idiot either.

Ambrose is talking about me. About the deal that saved my life when I was standing on death's doorstep, posed to knock. I'd be dead without Beau. If Ambrose's words, tone, expression and body language are anything to go by, he'd prefer it that way.

Part of me wants to step in front of Beau and shield him from Ambrose's disapproval but Beau is standing rigid beside me, eyes on the… I assume Ambrose is a demon.

Aside from his odd eye color and the sharp fangs I caught a flash of when he approached, he looks like a very attractive human—like Beau with his glamor. Maybe he's a vampire. It would explain why he pulled me close and sniffed me like a dog might a medium rare steak.

As far as I know, vampires have no interest in souls and Ambrose mentioned mine being more than enough to make up for the mistake Beau made ten years ago. If only he knew…

I lay a hand of silent support on Beau's spine. He doesn't pull away but doesn't acknowledge me either as he glares at his… friend. If Ambrose can really be called a friend.

Ambrose is the first to break the stalemate. His shoulders slump and he sighs. "I'm sorry. I just don't understand. This… attachment you have to humanity—" His gaze cuts to me, a little colder than it was when we were introduced, before returning to Beau. "It only hurts you in the long run."

I can't argue with Ambrose's assessment, not when I saw the pain in Beau's expression earlier today. Having to leave one place for another every few decades… His life really has been a series of goodbyes.

Is there a string of dead lovers standing behind him? Am I doomed to join their ranks, be nothing more than a specter haunting him across all of time? The last thing I want to be for Beau is another unavoidable heartbreak. How can I be anything else when he has forever and I only have another fifty years—maybe seventy if I get really lucky?

"It was nice to meet you, Ambrose," I lie—nothing about meeting him has been nice, not the way he spoke to Beau, or the way he glares at me as I wrap my arm around Beau's waist, pull him against my side and look down. "But it's late. Should we head home?"

Beau exhales and nods. "Stay out of trouble, Rose."

Ambrose huffs and shoves his hands into his pockets, rocking back on his heels. "Same. Not that you'll listen." He shakes his head. "You never do. Just… take care of yourself."

I draw Beau away with a polite smile. As we round the corner there's a sharp tug under my ribcage. Traveling with Beau is easier now; he doesn't have to cling to keep me upright. Everything is dark and topsy-turvy for a long second before my feet land on solid ground.

It was dark when we left Outer Banks but in New York sunlight streams through my apartment window, illuminating the hardwood floor and the pile of clothes in the chair. I step away from Beau, who shoves his hands into his pockets and hunches his shoulders.

"I'm sorry about—"

"Why was Ambrose so upset about our deal?" I interrupt. I don't want Beau to apologize for his friend's behavior. He's not responsible for anything Ambrose said or did. All I need is for him to explain what just happened. Why did Ambrose act that way? "He called it a debacle. He was... disappointed. Incredulous."

"What kind of demon accepts a favor in exchange for anything?"

Beau sighs and pushes his fingers through his hair. "You have to understand. When a demon makes a deal, they convert a portion of their life force into a type of magic that works to fulfill the agreement. The magic, and the dealmaker's soul, return to the demon upon death, growing our power and extending our life force when we... consume the soul."

Consume the soul? I open my mouth to ask for clarification but stop. I'm probably better off not knowing some things. What I do know is Beau has no claim to my soul. *Good health in return for a favor.*

When I die... Beau will get nothing, and while I'm alive— "Ambrose is mad because... a portion of your life force is sustaining our deal. I'm sucking the life out of you. *Literally.*"

Beau crosses the floor and takes hold of my upper arms. His eyes aren't as human as the rest of him as his fingers dig almost painfully into my skin. "Not enough to matter. Not really. For every year of good health you get, I lose a year but I have *a lot* of years under my belt, more than any one person can hope to live, Max. Ambrose is making mountains out of molehills."

Is he? Beau is losing years off his life, years he's just... giving to me, for nothing. And yeah, maybe he does have more years to spare than any one person can hope to live but . . how is it fair to him that he gets nothing but scorn from his so-called friends for doing so much for me?

No. No. Absolutely not.

"Beau—"

He shakes me, gently but noticeably. "No. Listen. Now is not the time to be a martyr, Max. I knew what I was doing ten years ago and given the chance, I'd make the same deal."

I open my mouth, then close it. What can I say? He knew exactly what he was agreeing to, even if I didn't, when he saved my life and I don't regret making a deal with him. How can I? I've lived a healthy and well fulfilled life. But it's been ten years—a decade in which I have taken from him over and over again without any means to repay him. Aside from the favor I owe him.

"I don't want to keep taking years from you." Even if he has more time to spare than the whole of humanity, I don't want to be the reason anyone sneers at Beau with contempt or disapproval—not Ambrose or any other demon. He deserves better than that. I care about him too much to be the reason he's a pariah among his own people. "How is our deal fulfilled?"

He steps away, hands up as if to ward me off as he shakes his head, blonde hair tumbling around his ears. "No, Maxton. Not happening."

What does he mean, no?

We made a deal. At some point he has to collect.

I take a step towards him. "The magic will return to you once our deal is done, right?"

Once the magic returns to Beau, no one will have a reason to judge him. Or, well… they might because he won't have my soul, but at least he won't be sacrificing magic for me anymore.

"It's not that simple, Max." He looks away, eyes downcast, a sad tilt to his mouth. "When our deal is done and the magic returns to me—" His throat bobs as he swallows. I wait, giving him time to gather his thoughts. "You'll get sick again, as sick as you were the night we made the deal. Maybe even worse."

"Oh." I exhale and stumble towards the sofa, where I collapse. With the deal fulfilled and the magic gone, the cancer will come back and… "I'll die. Of cancer." The same cancer his magic cured.

Beau drops to his knees in front of me. His eyes are human again, soft and understanding as he rubs my thighs. "Ambrose and the other demons don't understand because soul collection is… it's like a game to them, a competition where the winner gets nothing more than bragging rights."

Is it not like that for Beau? Does he really not care about the magic and the years he's losing just to keep me alive? Do I have the right to be upset with his choice when it's *his* choice? If he's willing to sacrifice to keep me alive I should be grateful, not angry.

I hate it though. The way Ambrose treated him because of me.

I cup his smooth jaw in my palm. "How can I ever repay you?"

I don't want to die, but still. There must be something I can do.

He turns his face into my hand, pressing a kiss to the center of my palm before meeting my gaze. Something warm unfurls behind my ribcage. Loving him would be so easy, if I thought it wouldn't break his heart in the long run.

I'm already in love with him. Maybe I always have been. My love will destroy him; his magic can't keep me alive forever. Then what? He spends who knows how long mourning me? No. I can't ever tell him how deeply I care for him, can I?

"You still owe me a favor. After you've lived a long and healthy life I'll collect what little magic remains."

"How can that be enough?"

"It just is, Max. I don't need anything else."

"Maybe not." I pull him into my lap; his knees fall on either side of my thighs as he rests his hands on my shoulders. I encircle his waist with my hands and draw him against my chest. "But I need to not be another heartbreak you nurse long after I'm dust. I don't want to be another ghost that haunts you."

How can I be anything else?

Beau's smile is soft as he presses his forehead against mine. "Most demons have forgotten heartbreak is a privilege of the human condition. The pain reminds us we're alive, and leading lives worth living. When you are long gone—dust as you say—even the ghost of you will be better than nothing."

Fuck. This demon... I slide my hand into his hair and cup the back of his head before pulling him down. Our mouths slot together. Beau melts against my chest and in the next instant his tongue splits against mine. When I pull back his eyes are black with green slits, horns curled around his head and black spider veins extending down his arms. Sharp nails scratch over my scalp.

Our problem still isn't solved but a solution isn't going to magically appear either. We will figure something out. A way for me to live the long, healthy life Beau wants for me without constantly taking his magic. Not today. Today—

My stomach growls and Beau pulls away with a soft laugh. "We missed dinner."

"I can order dinner."

"No. There's somewhere I wanted to take you. Everything else can wait." Beau climbs out of my lap and offers me his hand. I take it and he helps me to my feet. My apartment disappears and suddenly we're standing in front of a door with a pair of foxes playing in a flower field etched into the glass. The world doesn't spin. My knees don't knock together. Beau pulls the door open and the scent of food assaults my senses as we step inside.

A young man with fluffy ears—mostly a warm red, but tipped with white—greets us just inside with a wide smile. "Welcome to For Fox Sake. Just two? Booth or table?"

For Fox Sake...

"Booth, please." Beau's shoulder presses against mine as he squeezes my hand. The young man spins on his heels and snatches up two menus before leading us through a cluster of tables and towards the back wall. He sets the menus down and steps back, pulling a pen and pad from his pocket as I slide in next to Beau.

"I'm Kit, and I'll be serving you tonight. Do you know what you'd like to drink?"

What do they *have* to drink? I glance down at the menu. Right away I notice there are a couple of items that are clearly meant for a more diverse palate than mine, but most of the meals sound pretty normal.

"Coke," Beau says.

"I'll have the same."

"Be right back." Kit scampers away. When he returns with our drinks, we place our orders—a hamburger with fries for me and chicken and rice with a side of vegetables for Beau.

I slide my arm around Beau's shoulder once we're alone. "How long have you known Ambrose?"

He hums and leans into my side. "Long enough to regret meeting him."

I laugh under my breath. "He seems to uh… care about you, in his own unique way."

Maybe he went about saying it the wrong way, but he was clearly concerned.

"I guess," Beau says, picking at a scratch on the table. "He's not usually such an asshole. Just… recently."

"Every friend has their moments."

Leland is my best friend—I'd die for him, and him for me. Yet, we've had periods when we stopped talking or came to blows because one of us crossed the line. When your best friend is prone to call you on your bullshit, and you do the same when needed, there's bound to be some friction. It doesn't mean you love them any less. Just that you want to strangle them from time to time.

Kit appears beside the table with plates in hand. "Anything else?"

Beau glances at me and I shake my head. "We're good. Thanks."

I reach for my burger as Kit leaves to tend to other tables. My stomach grumbles again and I take my first bite, moaning around the flavor explosion in my mouth. Is everything in Outer Banks destined to taste delicious? Plus, the service here is amazingly fast. We only ordered minutes ago. Magic for the win.

Beau digs into his food and before long our plates are empty. Kit drops a ticket off on the table but before I can grab it Beau drops a couple gold coins on top. If I ever want to pay for our meal, I'll have to find a way to convert the paper money I have into the gold coins they use here. Or buy Beau dinner in New York.

CHAPTER
THIRTEEN
BEAU

Despite the unpleasant encounter with Ambrose, the day with Max ends on a high note. He's still concerned about the magic that's sustaining his life when I drop him off at home, but other than reassuring him it's not a big deal—at least not to me—there isn't much I can do. I refuse to ask him for a favor until he's old and on his deathbed.

And when that happens…

I pause in the middle of undressing.

There is a way to end the deal so Max survives. He won't die of cancer or old age. In fact, he'd have his own magic, the same kind of magic I've possessed since I died and managed to escape the demon who intended to consume me.

It's an extreme measure. Possibly unfair in every way because eventually, if Max agrees to my so-called favor, he'll have to disappear. His family and friends can never know. One day, he will have to simply walk out of their lives and never look back. Aside from maybe Leland. The loudmouth human already knows about the parahuman community. Even if he didn't, if Max simply vanished into thin air Leland would search the world over for him—twice.

I pull my shirt over my head and check the time in New York.

It's not that late, just barely eight at night now. Max works tomorrow, he's probably getting ready for bed considering our long day but… if I can keep him from stressing for even a second, isn't it better to just… pop back over? I can at least ask what he thinks.

With barely a thought, I'm outside Max's door and a moment after I knock, he answers, bare chested, hair wet and dripping. I swallow around the sudden lump in my throat even as my eyes slip lower. No one looking at him would think once upon a time he was sick.

"Beau." He pulls the door further open and steps back. "Is everything okay?"

"Yeah." I clear my throat. "Everything is fine. Better than fine." I step into his apartment and shut the door behind me. "I think I found a solution to our… dilemma." I rub my hands down my thighs and sit on the edge of his sofa. Max follows, dropping down beside me. His hand slides into mine and I twine our fingers together as I search his face. "Do you remember how I told you before demons don't reproduce like humans?"

He frowns before he nods. "It's why you don't have a belly button in your demon form."

"Demons are…" How best to explain it without freaking him out? "We all start as humans. Humans who made a deal with a demon." I wet my bottom lip as Max's eyes widen, and his hand tightens around mine. "Sometimes, a collected soul escapes before it can be consumed. When that happens, they don't return to the soul cycle. They can't.

"But souls can't die—not unless they're consumed in some manner. So those of us who escape sometimes become… more." I tighten my hand around his and search his face to be sure he's still following along.

He nods for me to continue.

"You have to understand, it's a half-life," I whisper, my voice cracking around the confession. "Just because a soul can't die without being consumed doesn't mean it can't waste away. Become an echo of the last life they lived. In order to avoid that the escaped soul has to consume other souls, take another's life force to sustain their own. The more souls consumed, the less chance of becoming an echo."

Max is silent for a long moment and for the first time in what feels like forever I hold my breath as I wait for him to speak.

"So," his voice is slow and tentative as he brushes his thumb back and forth over my knuckles, "you escaped the demon you made a deal with and in order to not become an echo, you started consuming other souls?"

I nod and bite my bottom lip. He doesn't sound disgusted, just curious. "The moment you consume your first soul, you become a demon—weak, still in danger but the more souls you consume, the more the magic builds in you and eventually, you escape the soul plain and come back here as a full-fledged demon."

"I don't understand how this helps us," Max says, brow furrowing.

I take a slow but deep breath. "My favor—" Max's eyes widen and he shakes his head. I pause and think how to word it so the magic doesn't get the wrong idea. "If I decided to collect it, would you... would you want to become a demon? You'd never get sick, never die. It's not an easy life but... it's not all terrible either. And... I'd be there with you, every step of the way."

He opens his mouth before closing it. I let him sit with his thoughts.

A decision like this shouldn't be rushed. What I'm asking of him isn't a simple thing. It's... It's asking for forever when we've barely been dating a month.

"What about my family? Leland?" Max asks.

"Eventually, you'd have to cut contact. With your family, at least. The less people who know the truth, the better. Leland—" I shrug as I try not to laugh. "Let's be honest. He'd never just let you go."

Max huffs as he settles into the sofa. "No. He's just crazy enough to open the gates of Hell and send a search party if I vanished." He runs his fingers through his damp hair, scattering water droplets as he bites his bottom lip. "How long does it take? I mean... I'd have to die first. You'd collect the favor and—" Max's voice cracks and he swallows a couple of times as his hand shakes in mine "—and I'd die. Of cancer?"

"No." I scoot towards him, kneeling on the sofa at his side. "Depending on the favor I ask, it would be quick and painless. You would die but... not after weeks of suffering. And time moves differently on the soul plain. What feels like weeks or months there might be hours or days here. When I... My mother was still alive, still mourning my death by the time I was strong enough to leave the soul plain. No one would need to know you're not human anymore."

"Oh, Beau." Max curls his hand around the nape of my neck and pulls me down. I lie against his solid chest, tucking my face into his neck as I take a slow breath. His heat soothes a cold, endlessly hollow part of me. "You still remember being human?"

"It's the one lifetime I can't forget." I squeeze my eyes closed. No matter how many lives I've lived and subsequently forgotten, my first life as a human is one I can't forget. No matter how hard I try. And I have tried.

"Do you want to talk about it?" Max asks, combing his fingers gently through my hair.

I sigh. Considering I'm asking him to give up his life as a human, it's only fair I talk about my time as one. "The world was only as big as how far I could see. And there wasn't much to see. Mountains to the east. An endless body of water to the west. Our village survived on fish and wheat. Life was... hard, made harder by my father. He wasn't a kind man, but he kept us fed and sheltered. A stranger came one day, which was rare back then. He was kind—charming—so the village elder let him stay."

I brush my finger up and down Max's stomach, circle his belly button, play in his happy trail, and get lost in a time so long ago nothing remains of my small fishing village. It's lost to history—a forgotten place that may as well never have existed for all that's known about it.

"I was twelve, healing from a particularly nasty beating, avoiding going home because I knew when I did, I'd only be beaten again, when the stranger found me playing near the boats. He offered me a share of his food, spoke to me like I mattered, asked what happened. I told him, and he said he could make it so my father never hurt me or anyone else in my family, for a price to be paid at a later date. I told him anything. Whatever he wanted."

My laugh is dry and unhappy. I was a hurt child, with no idea what I was agreeing to, and maybe that was the point. To the demon who collected my soul I was an easy mark, a snared rabbit, willing to chew my own leg off in a bid to survive, never realizing I was dooming myself.

"My dad never raised his hand to any of us after that day. Life was good—everything I wanted it to be. Until shortly after my twenty-second birthday." I squeeze my eyes closed and breathe through my nose as that day flashes before me. "It was a bad week all around. A storm was coming. Dad had been on edge but he hadn't hurt us in years so it wasn't anything to be concerned about. Then one day, I came back empty handed from a hunt. He lost it in a way he hadn't in a decade." Max's arm tightens around me as I take a deep breath. "Beat me nearly to death. I ended up dying from my wounds anyway."

A slow, painful death, in which I suffocated as my lungs filled with blood.

"The demon met me on the soul plain. Until then, I'd forgotten all about him. But seeing him—hungry, and excited—I knew. I knew everything was his fault so I ran, managed to get away. It felt like forever until I left my hiding place. I was weak and tired when I saw one soul consuming another and… And I knew then what I had to do."

"I'm so sorry, Beau," Max whispers into my hair. His hand is warm on the back of my neck when he pulls me closer and brushes a chaste kiss against my temple. "I'm so fucking sorry. None of what happened is your fault."

"When a deal is almost fulfilled, the magic wanes. My dad had been on edge because the magic was fading. He really was a monster. The magic just… leashed him—like you muzzle a dog —and as soon as it was gone, he did what vicious animals do. Attack."

"The rest of your family?" Max asks, his voice tentative, as if he already knows the answer. Maybe he does. It's not a happy ending.

"My sisters were all married and safe from him by that point. Not from their own husbands though, who weren't any kinder. My older brother left the village years beforehand. He could never quite forgive our father. I never saw him again. And my mother—she stayed until he eventually killed her too."

What choice did she have? She was his wife, and in those days, that meant he owned her—like one might own a cat now. And me—I was already dead to her. She'd have chased me away, fearing I was a demon wearing her son's face, if I revealed myself. She wouldn't have been wrong.

"I terrorized him after she was gone," I whispered. It's a secret I've kept even from my closest friends. "Drove him mad. He took his boat out one day and never came back. I hope he drowned."

"Good." Max tugs me into his lap until I'm straddling his hips. "Death is the least of what he deserved."

I wrap my arms around his neck and exhale, letting the tension bleed from my shoulders. My family is long dead. Just because I won't ever forget them, doesn't mean I have to let their memory haunt me. Hurt me. Even if it still does from time to time. Like now. Everything hurts a little less as I listen to Max's steady heartbeat and he runs his work-rough hands over my body.

For the first time, the only lifetime I've never been able to forget doesn't feel like the only life that has ever truly mattered.

This life matters. Max matters.

I don't want to lose him. I can't.

It will destroy me in a way nothing ever has.

N o.

That's what the answer should be. Absolutely not. Dying only to be reborn as a demon is an insane idea. But… with Beau in my lap—head on my chest, warm breath on my neck, cold hands tucked between our bodies—after having shared what is probably the most traumatic time of his life, the only thing I want to do is say yes.

Yes, I'll give up my humanity if it means an eternity with Beau. A half-life with him is better than no life at all. If I can give him forever, spare him another heartbreak, why wouldn't I?

And really, I should've died ten years ago. It's because of the demon resting in my arms I got to grow up, have a life at all. He gave me ten years that I never would've had otherwise. That I *shouldn't* have had, because he got nothing out of it—not even the favor we agreed upon since he clearly has no intention of ever collecting, unless it's so I can join him in eternity.

I know without a doubt, even if I turn his offer to become a demon down, he'll continue to let me use his magic for another ten, twenty, even thirty years. The rest of my life. When the time comes and I'm in my last minutes, knowing him, he'll just wish me the best in my next life.

Beau will support whatever choice I make. That, more than anything, makes me want to choose him.

"I want to tell Leland first," I whisper in his hair. Beau pulls back and searches my face. "If something goes wrong he can…" What will Leland really be able to do? He's resourceful to be sure —the guy found a demon summoning ritual online when we were sixteen—but he's still as human as I currently am. Even so… "He should know. And he'll be there for my family."

Beau's eyes are soft and his smile is small as he cups my jaw and brushes his mouth over mine. "There's no rush, Max. You don't have to decide today. It's just something to consider. An option for you, if you ever want to take that step."

I shake my head and grasp his wrist, turning my head to press a kiss to his palm. "I've decided."

It's not just about me not wanting to use Beau for his magic anymore—magic he needs to keep himself from becoming an echo.

Beau has been alone more often than not I suspect. Countless lives he's lived, and probably loved, only to always end up heartbroken and with nothing—no one. I'm going to make sure he's never alone again.

Now, tomorrow, a year from today, it doesn't matter when it happens. So long as Beau is aware I'm willing to do whatever's required to become a demon, and stop draining his magic in the process.

"Are you sure?"

I've never been more sure of anything.

"I want to talk to Leland, see my mom and dad, in case something goes wrong. Then, we can do it."

"Max…" Beau presses his forehead to mine as he exhales. "Doing it now gives you fifteen, maybe twenty years before you'll have to disappear. Your parents will still be alive then. But if you wait a few more years, they might…" His eyes are endless pools of sadness as he trails off and pushes his fingers through my hair.

I understand what he can't bring himself to say.

If I wait, my parents might be dead by the time I have to disappear. I won't leave them heartbroken and with more questions than answers if I put off becoming a demon for the time being.

Is it fair to make Beau wait, to continue to drain his magic for another five, maybe ten years? And what happens when it's time for him to disappear, in another decade or so?

I sigh and close my eyes.

There's no easy answer. No easy solution.

Maybe I'm being rash—leaping without looking, like Leland is so prone to do—by deciding to surrender my humanity to be with Beau after less than a month of dating but... this feels right. Like ten years ago, the universe arranged our lives so both of us would be in the right place, at the correct time, to eventually end up here. In a place where I could love Beau, and he could love me in return. What are the odds Leland would attempt to summon a demon, and my hot-as-sin night nurse actually *be* a demon, after all?

"If you'd taken my soul in exchange for good health ten years ago, what would happen?" I ask. Beau swallows and looks away. "The magic would have waned, right? And I'd slowly get sick again." His nod is small, his shoulders tense as his fingers dig into my skin. I take a deep breath and exhale slowly. "Relapse isn't unheard of." It's a known fact that if you get cancer once, you're more likely to get it a second time. "It's rare this far out but not impossible. And if I die slowly—"

"No, Maxton." Beau climbs out of my lap and moves away. "Just... no."

"Listen." I stand and follow. "It sounds horrible but it's a kindness, really. For everyone. I can wait a couple years but those are years you lose, and I don't. I can't keep doing that to you." It isn't fair. He's already done so fucking much for me, and it's risky too. How many souls does he have to consume, how much magic does he need, to avoid becoming an echo?

"Plus," I continue as I come to a stop in front of him, "even when my parents are gone, my brother won't be. And what am I going to do? Put it off for another fifteen, twenty years? I'll be an old man by then, Beau. If… if I die of cancer, it will break their hearts but they won't spend the rest of their lives wondering what happened to me, if they'll ever see me again. They get to say goodbye."

He presses the heels of his hands into his eyes. "This was a horrible idea. I never should've said anything."

I grasp his wrist and pull his hands down. "It's my choice, isn't it?"

He made his choice ten years ago. I'm making mine now.

"Watching you slowly waste away was… it was torture, Max. And now—" His voice cracks; he sucks in a sharp breath and swallows several times. "It would be so much worse now. I'm not sure… I'm not sure I can watch you die like that."

I flatten his hand against my chest, over my beating heart, as I meet his watery gaze. "You said it's the nature of souls to leave one life and move on to the next to be reborn. The soul cycle, you called it." His nod is small as he draws a shaky breath. "This is only that, Beau. I'm not really dying. I'll be reborn as a demon. *With you.*"

He sucks in a sharp breath and stumbles forward, crashing against my chest. He shoves his fingers into my hair and pulls my mouth down to meet his. It's almost violent, the way he forces his tongue between my lips, but I grasp the backs of his thighs and yank him into my arms.

"I love you," he whispers against my mouth, like a confession. "I love you."

A sun's worth of warmth explodes behind my ribcage. "I love you. So fucking much."

Maybe it's crazy. I can't explain it. This thing between us

grew big and fast and out of control in a matter of weeks. It's true though. I love this demon. Now. Forever. If—No. *When* I become a demon, we will have an eternity together.

Beau wraps his legs around my waist. His nails scrape against my scalp as he slots his mouth over mine again. His tongue splits as soon as he slips into my mouth. I groan and tighten my hold on him, staggering towards my bedroom. He tugs on my hair, yanking my head back and licking a path down my throat as I kick my door shut.

"Clothes. Off." There are too many layers between us and I want them gone. I want Beau naked and sobbing with pleasure.

He wiggles out of my arms and rips his shirt over his head, throwing it away before kicking off his shoes. We shove our pants down at the same time. My cock slaps against my stomach, harder than it's ever been, leaking like a broken faucet. Beau drops to his knees, fists the base of my shaft, and swallows me down in one take.

"Fuck." I shove my fingers into his hair, gripping the soft strands as he moans around my cock. It shouldn't be as hot as it is—him on his knees, looking at me through damp lashes with his sharp teeth dangerously close to my cock. I should be terrified to have his mouth around me. But instead… holy fuck—

His mouth is hot and wet. The amount of suction he applies as he swallows around my shaft is enough to have me close to exploding in seconds. I pull him off my cock and to his feet before I reach the point of no return. His lips are slick and swollen, cheeks flushed, eyes wide and glassy. "Why—"

"Get on the bed," I rasp as I squeeze the base of my cock. "On your back."

He stumbles away, ass high and tight, right there for the taking as he does as I say. But tonight, I have something else in mind.

I grab the lube from my nightstand and hesitate over the condoms before looking at Beau. "Do we need protection?"

He shakes his head, sharp horns digging into my pillows, hair falling into his eyes before he shoves it backwards. "No. I can't get or transmit diseases. You're safe with me."

I swoop down, press my mouth against his, and push my tongue between his lips for a quick taste before pulling back. His mouth chases mine and he whines in protest, but I plant my hand on his chest to hold him down. "Hands above your head."

His eyelids droop as he lifts his arms and wraps his slender fingers through the wooden slats. Saliva pools in my mouth. My balls clench at the picture he makes—back arched, nipples swollen, abdomen tight, cocks hard, spread out on my bed waiting for my next command.

He's perfect.

I climb up beside him and pop the top on the lube. Beau's eyes never leave my face as I warm the slick between my fingers before tossing the bottle away.

"Watch."

His lips part and he pants for breath but his eyes never leave me. On my hands and knees, I turn, giving him a front row seat as I prep myself.

The first finger slips in easily. No resistance. No burn. Just a soft bloom of pleasure that throbs in my balls.

Beau's breathing is heavy, harsh and uneven in the otherwise silent room. His toes curl as his legs quiver beside me. I grunt as I add a second finger, quickly followed by a third.

It's been a long time since I bottomed but for this first time with Beau, I want to feel him inside of me, stretching me open and making me come apart on one of his cocks while I...

I squeeze my eyes closed and breathe through my nose, pulling my fingers free from my body before I make a mess of myself. Beau whimpers and I turn, grasping the longer, thicker cock and coating it in lube. He thrusts into my fist, arms and thighs quivering. "Max. Maxton."

"Easy." I toss my leg over his lap and brace my weight on my knees while holding his cock steady. Beau's eyes are wide, bright with desire, chest heaving. I can see the tips of his sharp teeth and forked tongue as our gazes meet and hold.

My heart is banging against my chest as if trying to escape as I line his cockhead up with my slick hole. A bead of sweat rolls down my temple. My skin is buzzing. Goosebumps pepper my thighs.

He moans, tossing his head back, squeezing his eyes closed, as I sink down, taking him into my body inch by slow inch. The pressure is exquisite and I gasp, my breath exploding out of me in a pleased rush, when he nudges the sensitive bundle of nerves inside of me.

Has anyone ever felt so damn good splitting me open?

"Max—I can't. I'm not—oh fuck. Wait. Wait." He shudders as he squeezes his eyes closed. Pre-cum leaks from his slit, pooling on his belly. My ass meets his hips and I plant my hands on his slender chest, holding still until his inhuman eyes meet mine.

"You good?"

After several minutes, he inhales a soft breath and nods. "You can move."

I roll my hips and tease a hard nipple with my thumb. His body tenses, every muscle pulling tight, as his hands spasm around the slats. The black spider veins that run under his pale flesh seem to pulse.

My balls draw up tight against my body as I find a steady rhythm. Beau arches against me, thrusting up to meet me as I fall down. Our cocks slide together, hot and hard and so fucking eager. An intense wave of pleasure rocks through me. I bow my head and capture his mouth as I tug on one of his nipples, roll it between my thumb and forefinger. His lips part and his tongue twists around mine.

"Max," he gasps against my mouth, breath hot on my chin. "My hands."

"Stroke us," I mutter.

He shoves his hands between our bodies, needing no further encouragement, and wraps his fist around our cocks. I groan and press my forehead against his cheek, heaving for breath. Having him inside of me, stretching me to the brink, his other cock lined up perfectly with mine, is like nothing I've ever felt before. Perfect. He drags his thumb over my leaking slit on the upstroke. I shift my hips forward, thrusting into his fist.

Beau turns his head, pressing his face into my throat. He lays a kiss on my pulse as his slick hands tighten around us. "I'm close."

"Come. I wanna feel you."

He whimpers and swells inside me, impossibly harder. I'm full to bursting as my hole clenches around him. His cock pulses—not just the one inside of me, but the one he has trapped against mine, too. Wet heat spreads between us as he slams home, as deep as he can possibly be, and cries out.

Pleasure sparks up my spine and I detonate. My cum mixes with his between us as he strokes me through my orgasm. The edge of my vision darkens and I collapse against Beau's chest, riding a wave of pleasure so extraordinary I can't catch my breath.

What just happened? How did we end up here? One minute we were talking about my past—and his possible future—then…

"I love you. So fucking much."

It's insane, isn't it? Not just the fact I feel the way I do—and admitted it out loud—but that Max feels and did the same. We barely know each other. I don't think the time we spent together when he was a sick child counts. Nothing about that time in our lives was romantic. Neither of us should feel this connected so fast, unless…

Was the witch who read Max's palm talking about me—about us? What did she say?

"And here, this is your love line. You'll have a happy love. Sweet. Understanding. A forever kind of love. Soulmates. A fated love. You've already met them."

Are Max and I…

Do demons even have soulmates?

Is that possible? If so, how?

"Okay?" Max climbs into bed, kisses behind my ear and tugs me into his arms, tossing a leg over my hip after throwing the cloth he used to clean us up in the hamper.

I hum, slide my arm around his waist, and curl against his chest. "Perfect."

"You seem lost in thought." He runs his hand up and down, pausing to stroke one of the dimples of Venus on my lower back. "You wanna talk about it?"

I sigh and tip my head back, leaving a kiss on his jaw. "Just… do you remember what the witch who read your palm said?" Max hums, his brow furrowing. "About your love line."

"Oh. Oh!" Max sits up, rolling me to my back. One hand lands beside my head, and he cups my jaw with his other. His smile blooms wild and free. "She said I already met my soulmate." I swallow around the sudden lump in my throat and look away. Max runs his thumb across my cheek and I meet his happy gaze. "You think maybe she was talking about you?"

I open my mouth and close it. Who else could she have been talking about? Max isn't involved with anyone else. We might not know each other as well as two people who declare themselves in love should, but I know without a doubt Max isn't the kind of guy to lead one man on while sleeping with another.

And what other explanation is there for this sudden, all-consuming thing between us?

"Maybe?" I eventually choke out.

"It doesn't matter what she says one way or the other—I want to be with you—but… we could ask her." His gaze slips to the window. It's dark out, well past midnight in Outer Banks now. We've had a long day. It feels like more time has passed than actually has. Was it really only this morning Max was thinking of faking a heart attack to get me out of work? "In the morning."

I nod and he lays beside me, dragging me into his arms. Within minutes, I feel the tug of sleep and let it pull me under. I wake with a gasp, back arching, cocks rock hard and leaking with Max between my spread thighs. His laugh is deep but soft as he peers up at me from beneath his lashes.

"Finally awake?" His lips are swollen and spit slick.

"Max," I groan as he finds the soft nub inside of me and strokes it.

"This okay?" He licks a stripe up one of my cocks before sucking the head between his lips. I whine and bend my knees as I roll my hips, attempting to get deeper in his mouth.

He chuckles and the sound sends vibrations down my shaft even as he continues to move his slick finger in my hole. My neglected cock flexes against his cheek, leaving a smear of pre-cum behind, and he releases the one in his mouth to take the other between his lips with a needy hum.

"Max… Max—I need—" My voice cracks and he pops off my cock, surges up my body and slots his mouth over mine. I groan and shove my fingers into his hair, yanking on the strands as a third finger joins the two already in my body.

Prep isn't necessary. He could take me with none, dry as a bone and it wouldn't hurt. It might be uncomfortable but I'm durable enough to handle a hard, fast fuck. The fact he took the time to take care of me means the world.

I lick into his mouth, whine at the taste of myself on his tongue before pulling away. My chest heaves as I press my forehead against his chin and look down to watch his fingers disappear into my hole. As nice as it feels, it's not enough, not by a long shot. "Fuck me. Please. I need you."

"Shit," Max swears under his breath, pulls his fingers free and grasps the base of his shaft. I draw my knees back, pulling them against my chest as he sits back on his knees. "You're sure?"

"You won't hurt me," I promise. At this point, I would say the same thing if he *could* hurt me. I'm that desperate. "Fuck me."

Max lines his cock up with my hole and thrusts. He sinks into my body to the hilt, hitting just the right spot to have me crying out, my back arching. Does he have any idea how good it feels to have him inside of me?

Last night was amazing. I enjoyed every second of Max riding my cock, getting lost in his own pleasure as I was helpless to do anything but watch until he gave me permission to stroke us. But this… this is a whole other level. I don't mind topping but bottoming has always been more pleasurable for me. It's never felt this good before though.

"Harder, Max."

He grabs the backs of my thighs, tilts my hips up and slams into me without hesitation or question. The show of trust is as heady as everything else about this moment. His balls slap against my ass. The headboard bangs against the wall. If he has neighbors, I hope they have earplugs.

I fist the bedsheet, nails tearing through the thin fabric. Max doesn't slow, doesn't seem to care about his sheets at all as he tunnels into my body at just the right angle to have me heaving for breath, cocks leaking.

A bead of sweat drips off his nose as his eyes meet mine. They're bright with lust but soft and warm, almost reverent. I reach down to take myself in hand but Max is there, slapping my hand away, wrapping one of his around both my cocks. He strokes from base to head, hand matching the rhythm of his hips.

It's too much. A pleasure overload. I'm gasping for breath, not sure what to do with my hands as I first clench the sheets again then shove them into my hair and squeeze my eyes closed. Lights, like fireflies on a dark night, flash behind my eyelids. My stomach quivers.

Everything outside of us doesn't matter. How can it when Max is all I truly need to be happy?

"Max. Max." His name is a broken chant, falling from my lips like a prayer for salvation. I'm so close to coming when he leans forward and slots his mouth over mine. His tongue parts my lips as the fingers of his free hand bite into my hip. If I was human I'd bruise from the force he's using. I'd wear every mark proudly.

"Can I come in you?" he whispers against my mouth before nipping at my bottom lip. I can't find the words to tell him he can do anything he wants to me. I'm his. "Beau," his voice is sharp and strained. "Tell me."

"Yes," I gasp as I clench his shoulders and roll my hips. "Do it. Fuck me. Fill me." He groans, the hand around my cocks tightening as he strokes me faster, pushing me towards oblivion. "I'm close."

"Come on, sweetheart. Come for me." Max buries his face in my neck, licks and nips at my throat as he slams into me.

I slide my hands down his back, palm his ass and hold on as he makes a solid attempt to fuck me through the mattress.

His teeth sink into my shoulder, not hard enough to break flesh, or even leave a mark, if such a thing were possible, but more than enough to have my hole clenching and my cocks pulsing between us.

He groans and slams into me, my body rocking towards the headboard, before holding himself there as his cock jerks, fills me with wet heat.

Pleasure continues to roll through me as he slowly rolls his hips, fucking his cum deeper into my body as if by doing so he can make it a part of me, before he eventually softens and falls out.

I'm still panting for breath, trying to catch my bearings when Max sits back, grabs my hips and rolls me to my stomach without a word.

"Max—" He cups my ass and spreads my cheeks before I can ask what he's doing. The hot swipe of his tongue over my loose hole has me seeing stars as I push back to meet his mouth. My cocks twitch against the ruined sheet.

The sounds he makes as he feasts on my body are hungry. Mine are helpless. He licks and sucks, cleans his cum from inside of me, before rolling me over and claiming my mouth once more.

The taste of him is shared between us. I suck it from his tongue, swallow it, and he licks it from my mouth before giving it back as he holds my face in the palms of his hands, until the taste of his cum is nothing more than a memory.

I sigh against his lips, tangling my fingers in his hair and holding him close. He sucks on my bottom lip before pressing his forehead against mine, panting for breath. "How was that?"

My laugh is weak as I brush my nose against his. "Five stars; ten-ten would do again."

He pecks me on the nose as he grins. "Good morning."

"Good morning." I sit up and he pulls back to give me room. There's a pleasant hum, like the air just after a hard thunderstorm, in my body as I stretch my arms over my head.

Max combs his fingers through my hair, brushing over the base of one of my horns. It's a feather light touch I feel in my cock but ignore as he asks, "Hungry?"

"I could eat."

He slides out of bed. "I called my dad, explained that I need a few days off."

A few days so he can talk to Leland about becoming a demon and get his affairs in order before dying of cancer.

I swallow and nod, not sure what else to say. It's his choice. As much as I hate the idea of him dying of the same sickness I saved him from, I won't stand in his way if he thinks it's the right thing to do.

"Do you still want to see the witch this morning?" he asks.

I exhale and climb out of bed, trailing after him as he slips into his bathroom. "Yeah. She might be able to offer a better solution."

At the very least, she can tell us if we're soulmates. Fated.

If we aren't... I'll cross that bridge when we get to it.

Max turns the water on and reaches for me. His arms curl around my waist and I lean into his chest, tucking my head under his chin.

With previous lovers who attempted to hold me like this, I pushed them away, hating the reminder of how small and weak I appear. With Max, I know how tall I am isn't something he's ever considered. He just wants me close, and this is the best way for that to happen.

I press a kiss to his collarbone and pull away before we step into the shower. Unlike the last time we showered together, there are no hand jobs—we trade kisses and shampoo bottles.

Max bends to wash his legs, and pauses. "Goddamn it."

"What?" I ask, trying my best to suppress a smile.

"Do you wash your legs?" He does his best to mimic my voice and I can't help but laugh, the sound loud in the enclosed space, echoing around us.

"Not sorry," I tease as I take the loofah and wash my legs before passing it back to him. He shakes his head and scrubs his lower body before we rinse off and step out of the shower.

I dry and wait for him to dress, then snag my clothes and his hand. With a single step, we're in my apartment and Max follows me to my room, watching as I yank a clean shirt over my head.

"Will I be able to teleport like you after I become a demon?" he asks.

"Probably. It's not magic unique to me." Most demons can move from place to place with hardly a thought. It makes collecting and consuming souls easier.

"Will…" He pauses and looks away. "Will I still look like me, when I come back from the soul plain?"

I lace my fingers through his. "You will, when you decide to use a glamor. The magic that hides you will choose the easiest method, and that's making you appear like you did in the last life your soul lived."

His hand tightens around mine. "Do all demons look the same?"

I shake my head as my glamor settles over me. "No. You might share some characteristics—horns, clawed hands and feet, possibly a tail or even wings—but your manifestation will be unique to you."

Max exhales. "I guess I'll have to wait and see. We have a witch to visit."

CHAPTER
SIXTEEN
MAXTON

The door to The Bone Tarot opens before I have a chance to touch the knob. Beau steps in ahead of me. Now that I know how it feels, I can tell magic is heavy in the air in the empty shop. The woman from before—the one who read my palm—is standing behind the counter, a deck of glowing cards in her hands.

"Back again." Her smile is welcoming. "How can I help you?"

It's a good question, for which I have no answer. Can she really tell if Beau and I are soulmates? If so, how? And… really what does that even mean, to be soulmates?

Beau's hand tightens around mine. "What kinds of readings do you offer?"

She comes out from behind the counter, tucking her cards out of sight in the folds of her flowing green skirt. "I tailor my readings based on my customers' needs. Are you interested in individual or joint readings?"

"Joint," Beau says.

"Last time I was here—" I pause and glance at Beau. What if she wasn't talking about him? Do I really want to know? It won't change anything. Even if he isn't mine, I choose him. That has to matter more than a foretold connection. "You mentioned I'd already met my soulmate. A fated love?"

She leans against the counter and nods. Blonde strands of hair fall from her bun and curl around her pointed chin. Freckles dot her cheeks and the bridge of her nose like constellations in the night sky. "What do you know about soulmates?"

"Not a lot," I admit. Until she read my palm I didn't believe in soulmates at all. They were just a fairytale concept for romance novels.

Her nose wrinkles. She sighs and sounds… disappointed. "You and everyone else."

I step closer to Beau, who presses his shoulder against mine. No matter what she says, we're leaving together to meet Leland so I can talk to him about my plan.

She crosses one leg over the other. "Every soul has a soul family. These are souls that you meet across each lifetime. Each takes a different form, and serves a different purpose, but they are essential to your soul's development. Soul families rarely change unless something happens to sever the threads that bind." Her gaze moves to Beau before coming back to me. "Contrary to popular belief, you can have more than one soulmate."

She steps away from the counter and tucks her hands into hidden pockets. "They aren't always romantic partners. Sometimes they're our closest friends. People we have an instant connection with that goes deeper than DNA or circumstances."

Like what Beau and I share. Or Leland and I.

"Most people, when they refer to a soulmate, are talking about their fated mate. An all-encompassing love that is deeply emotional and physical."

"Can you tell if two people are soulmates—fated mates?" Beau asks, getting to the heart of the reason we're here.

She nods. "Most of the time. There are circumstances that make it impossible to know. Unfortunately, because demons are souls who abandoned their soul cycle, and thus their soul family, the threads that connect them have been severed."

So… there's no way Beau is my soulmate? My fated mate?

His shoulders fall and his hand loosens around mine.

No. No. I tighten my grasp, refusing to let go.

She's wrong. Even if she's not, I simply don't care.

"Nothing's changed." Beau's gaze meets mine as I speak; I cup his jaw in my free hand. "So what if she can't see if you're my soulmate. That doesn't mean you're not, right?" I glance at the witch but don't give her time to answer—I really don't give a shit if she agrees or not. I look at Beau.

"Your ties might be gone but you're still a soul, and you had a soul family at one point. Who can say we weren't part of the same family, that we aren't fated mates who just… lost each other for a while?"

"He's right," the witch says. "You're a lost soul, but still a soul. Chances are you've crossed paths with members of your soul family each time they've been reborn, but because you're no longer connected by the threads of fate, you'd drift apart unless you were bound in some other way."

Another way. Like…

"We made a deal when I was sick as a teenager," I blurt. She arches an eyebrow. "A favor in exchange for good health. Would that be enough?"

"Let's see." She holds her hands out. I step forward and place my hand in hers. If there's anything to see I want to see it.

Beau does the same. She closes her eyes and takes several deep breaths. Her eyes are white, lit from within, when she opens them, peering at us but not seeing us at all.

I look down. There are dozens of lines tethered to my hand, curling around my fingers, twisted around my wrist. They stretch through the walls, normally invisible threads that connect to other members of my soul family. Or so I assume.

The most important thread is the only red one, the one that

curls around my pinky. It extends to Beau, wrapping around his pinky, as well.

She releases our hands and steps back, taking several deep breaths. The light in her eyes fades, returning to the soft hazel they were when we entered the shop. "The Red Thread of Fate connects fated mates. Regardless of time, place or circumstances, those connected by the red thread are destined to always find each other, or spend a lifetime searching. It's the hardest thread to break. And the easiest to repair."

I grin as I look at Beau. "You were worried for nothing."

"What happens to the connection if both of us are demons?" Beau asks.

She hums and rocks back on her heels as her gaze goes distant. "I can't say for certain. If you"—her eyes move to me—"become a demon you cut ties to your soul family *but* considering one of you is already a demon, the connection might hold. Or even strengthen."

Even if it breaks altogether, we know the truth.

Beau is mine. I am his.

"Thank you," I say.

Beau slips his hand into his pocket. "What do we owe you?"

"A favor."

His hand tightens around mine before he nods. "Within limits. There are terms and conditions."

She seems to think about it before offering her hand. Beau lets mine go and they shake. "Good luck."

Beau's arm slides around my waist and he pulls me against his side. I still feel the sharp tug of leaving The Bone Tarot and Outer Banks behind altogether, but I'm not disoriented when we appear in Leland's office.

He screams, shoving his chair back, banging into the shelf behind him and throwing the pen in his hand at us before freezing. "Holy shit!" He slaps a hand over his chest. "What the fuck? Warn a guy!"

I grin, thinking of all the ways I'll be able to torture him once I'm a demon.

Revenge will be sweet.

I can't wait to make him regret every awful prank he ever played on me.

Leland frowns. "Why are you smiling like that?"

"Just imagining the future, and all the ways I'm going to make you suffer."

He scoffs and crosses his arms over his chest. "Bring it on."

He has no idea what he's in for.

I drop into one of the chairs across from his desk. "We need to talk." He opens his mouth and I hold up my hand. "It's important."

His face falls and he collapses into his chair. "Is the cancer back?"

I shake my head and reach across the desk, taking his hand in mine. "It's not cancer."

The last time I told him we needed to talk, that it was serious, we were sitting in my parents' backyard, feet dangling in the pool, and I told him I was sick, sick enough the doctors wanted to admit me to the hospital. But not one in New York.

He squeezes my hand. "What is it?"

"The deal I made with Beau—" I glance at him where he stands near the window, hands tucked into his pockets and shoulders hunched. "It's stealing his magic, taking years off his life to keep me alive."

Leland's head snaps to Beau. "You're dying."

Beau holds his hands up. "No. I'm fine. I've told Max I've got more years than he could possibly hope to live to spare."

I send him a sharp look. He's not helping my case. "The problem is our deal is… causing trouble for him in the demon community."

If I had to guess, I'd say Ambrose is only the tip of the

iceberg. Beau hasn't said as much but it would explain why he hasn't mentioned any other demons—not even Ambrose.

"And you're sure holy water doesn't work?" Leland asks, his gaze narrow and intent on Beau.

Beau laughs under his breath and comes away from the window. "Sorry to disappoint you. Demons aren't religious in nature."

Leland sighs. "So what are we going to do?"

This man. My best friend. I love him so fucking much.

I come to him with a problem, a problem that really has nothing to do with him, and his first course of action is to ask what we're going to do. Us. A team. Until death do us part.

Shit. If I become a demon, I'll be cutting the thread that binds him and me. Every thread that binds me to everyone important in my life will break, disappear, until I'm as lost a soul as Beau.

A warm hand lands on my shoulder. "You don't have to do this, Max. We're bound by the red thread—I'll always be able to find you."

I shake my head and swallow. "No. I want to do this."

Maybe it's insane considering Beau has said multiple times he has the years to spare, but I won't keep taking them just to die and abandon him one day.

"Do what?" Leland asks.

I take a deep breath. "When Beau asks me for a favor, the magic that binds us will fade. The cancer will come—"

Leland pushes out of his chair. "No. Fuck that." He glares at Beau as he rounds the desk. "You wouldn't do that."

"Leland," I catch his wrist to halt his forward movement. "It's not his choice. Or yours. Just listen."

He yanks his wrist from my hand and crosses his arms over his chest. His face is flushed, lips pressed into a firm line—angry. But I can also see the glassy shine of unshed tears in his eyes. I barely survived last time, and he did the impossible to make sure I did, so he has every right to be upset.

"When I die—" I start and Leland sucks in a sharp breath. "Beau is going to take me to the soul plain. While I'm there… I'll become a demon." He doesn't need to know the specifics. "It won't be for long—days, if not hours." I laugh but the sound is strained. "I'll be back in time to go to my own funeral."

"Max." Leland's voice is weak and broken. "You can't be serious."

I stand and grasp his shoulders. "This way is for the best. If I just do it without dying, in a few years when I have to disappear Mom and Dad will be heartbroken. They'll die never knowing what happened to me. And Kieran won't ever stop looking for me, hoping one day I'll come back. You understand that, don't you?"

He pulls me into his arms, pressing his face into my shoulder as I engulf him. "Can I count on you to be there for my family?"

He sniffs and bangs his head against my shoulder a couple of times before standing upright. "You owe me."

"Whatever you want."

It doesn't take as long as I thought it would—arranging Max's life so he can die after the magic that sustained him is gone.

The first thing he did—even before I cashed in on my favor—is sign everything over to Leland, who is heartbroken but doing his best to keep his head high, just like when he was a boy watching his best friend waste away.

Once Max is gone and a certain period of time has passed, Leland will quietly sell what can be sold and put the proceeds into the bank account attached to the new identity I've already arranged for Max.

The second thing he did, shortly after my magic no longer kept him healthy, was see his doctor who, after talking to him and examining the skin lesions and rashes that seemed to appear overnight, put a rush on a whole battery of tests. Within days, days where Max was tired and weak and skipped work much to his father's confusion, the doctor called.

Cancer.

An aggressive form of leukemia with a poor prognosis.

The last thing Max needs to take care of…

I wipe my sweaty hands off before opening the door and

stepping out into the midsummer heat. It's sad, damn near depressing, to think that by the end of summer Max will be too sick to leave his hospital bed. He'll miss the leaves changing, the first snowfall. And by the start of the holiday season—

Max isn't *really* dying. Life as he knows it is ending but a matter of hours or possibly days after his body stops functioning, he'll be reborn as a demon.

His soul cycle is ending though. This life will be the last one he experiences as a human. And for it to end on such a sad note… It's hard.

Max meets me in front of the car and slides his hand into mine. "Ready?"

"Not really."

Is anyone ever really ready to meet the parents of the person they're dating? Planning to turn into a demon in the very near future?

Not that I haven't met Julian and Hunter Grant. When I was Max's nurse I spoke with them plenty. Julian cried on my shoulders, giant heaving sobs of terror and helplessness, more than once. Hunter silently, with a tired but grateful smile that never reached his eyes, accepted countless cups of coffee.

Hopefully, they don't remember me as well as I remember them. If they do, Max and I decided I'll explain that my non-existent father, who I'm named after, was Max's nurse ten years ago. Unfortunately, he passed away in a car accident.

"They're going to love you." Max pulls me towards the front door. His steps are slower than usual; the cancer is already taking its toll.

The door opens as soon as we reach the first step. Julian, a little older, plumper around the middle, gray in her hair and wrinkles around her kind eyes but still lovely, smiles.

"You must be Beau," she says as she steps back to let us through the door. "You didn't tell me he was so handsome, Maxton."

Max's pale cheeks flush and I laugh before offering Julian my hand. "It's nice to meet you, Mrs. Grant. Max has told me a lot about you."

She waves my hand away and engulfs me in a tight hug. "Please, call me Jill. Everyone else does. Dinner will be done shortly."

We follow her into the kitchen and I inhale deeply, sucking down the scent of multiple spices. I don't *need* to eat, it's not imperative for my survival, but just because I don't need to doesn't mean I don't like to.

Food has come a long way since I was a human, and I'm not above indulging, even all these years later.

"Look who's here," Jill says, laying her hand low on Hunter's back. He's standing at the stove, adding meatballs to tomato sauce.

"Just in time." Hunter smiles over his shoulder, eyes running over Maxton. They dim slightly as he and Jill share a silent but loaded glance.

He looks so much like Max—same dark hair and kind eyes. They're the same height and share the same build. The hair at his temples is graying, and he has a well cared for beard now, but otherwise, he doesn't look as if he aged a day since the last time I saw him, standing in the hospital hallway, fist pressed to his mouth, crying silent tears of devastation because Max wasn't getting better.

And the doctors didn't think he would.

"This is Beau," Max says, pressing his shoulder against mine as he wraps his arm around my midsection. I lean into him, helping to silently support his weight. "We've been dating for a couple months now."

Hunter wipes his hands off on a kitchen towel and turns, extending one to me. "Nice to meet you, Beau. You can call me Hunter. None of that Mr. Grant business."

"Max says you're the family chef. It smells fantastic in here," I say as he releases my hand.

"I hope you're hungry. There's plenty." He turns back to the stove.

"I'm always hungry."

Hunter's shoulders shake as he chuckles and drains the pasta. "You're well matched." He nods to Max. "So is that one."

"Hey!" Max turns from the fridge, holding two bottles of water. I pretend not to notice his hands are shaking. "You're supposed to make me look good."

"No chance of that, love," Jill says as she pulls plates from the cabinet and forks from a drawer.

He huffs and hands me a bottle of water. I hide my smile behind a shallow sip.

"Leland's running late," Hunter says, gaze moving to the clock on the wall as his brow furrows. "Did something happen at the shelter?"

"He has a date tonight," Max lies, resting his shoulder against the wall.

"Good for him!" Jill says.

Hunter hums, finishes with the spaghetti and carries the pot to the table before returning to the oven to withdraw a sheet of garlic bread. We all sit down—Jill and Hunter on the right side of the table, Max and me on the left.

Conversation is easy and pleasant. Neither Jill nor Hunter goes out of their way to embarrass Max or interrogate me. They're as lovely as I remember, and I'm killing their son.

Not really, I have to remind myself. But they don't know that.

I blink in a bid to clear the burn in my eyes.

Guilt claws at my insides like a rabid animal.

"Are you alright, dear?" Jill's kind voice breaks into my thoughts.

I look up from my nearly empty plate. "Sorry." My smile is

weak at best. "Just got lost in thought." What else can I say? It's not up to me to explain.

Max's hand lands on my thigh under the table. "Do you need a minute? You don't need to be here for this, if you don't want to."

I shake my head and lay my hand on his. His skin is cold and dry. "No. I'm here. It's okay."

"Has something happened?" Hunter asks.

Max takes a deep breath, his fingers digging into my thigh. "I haven't been feeling well so I went to see my doctor. He sent me for some tests." His voice cracks and he clears his throat. Jill and Hunter look at one another before clasping hands on the table.

"The cancer—" Max stops and takes several deep breaths as Jill's eyes well with tears. She presses her hands against her mouth, shaking her head with a soft whine.

I look away and clench my jaw.

This is for the best. I know it is. It's what Max wants. So his parents don't have to live their last years with questions that have no answers. But why does it have to hurt so damn much? Not just me. But Max too.

These are good people, good parents who honestly love their son. They did so much for him, everything they possibly could, to give him a fighting chance as a teenager. And he survived the worst time of their lives, only to be here again, a decade later. Worse off than he was.

"What—" Jill's voice breaks as she turns into her husband's shoulder with a soft sob. Hunter wraps his arm around her, holding her close.

Max closes his eyes and takes a deep breath. I lace my fingers through his and squeeze. "The median survival rate is… low. Even with aggressive treatment, treatment that won't help in the long run. I've… I've decided to not drag it out, for any of us."

Hunter sucks in a sharp breath as a single tear runs down his cheek. "What—Whatever you need us to do."

"I've made arrangements with Leland for… for afterwards. He's going to handle everything." Max's hand shakes in mine as he clears his throat and blinks back tears. "Be here afterwards for —for you."

"How long?" Hunter's voice breaks around the question.

"Less than a year," Max manages to choke out. "Months, at best. Weeks, at worst."

I squeeze my eyes closed. Max curls his arm around my shoulder and I press my face into his chest as a sob claws its way up my throat. It's ridiculous. I know he's going to be reborn as a demon. But this… it hurts all the same.

I saved him once. Gave him ten years.

It doesn't feel like enough.

A second and third set of arms come around us as Hunter and Jill embrace their son, and me, silent tears streaming down their cheeks.

There is nothing I can say to ease their pain. I can't even begin to imagine how they feel.

Part of me wishes I'd never treated Max in the emergency department. He would've lived and died never knowing the truth, if not for that one moment in time. But another part is grateful I met him. He's my fated mate—the one soul in all of creation meant just for me.

Jill is the first to pull away. Her eyes are red and swollen, cheeks wet and flushed. "How about I change the sheets on your bed. You can stay the night." Max nods in agreement. We figured they'd want him close. We already packed an overnight bag. "Beau, are you staying?"

"I'm staying with Max," I tell her, holding her gaze, letting her know the only way I can that I'm here until the very end. And beyond. For him. Them, as well.

After Max is reborn I'll stop by and check on them for a while, make sure they're getting by okay. Then, eventually, I'll fade out of their life.

It wouldn't be fair to just abandon them suddenly after Max is gone. But, on the flipside, it wouldn't be fair to linger for years, reminding them their son is gone. That as far as they know, he'll never marry, never have kids. Never live the kind of life they probably imagined for him after he beat cancer the first time.

Jill's smile is weak, eyes sad enough to drown in, before she nods and turns away. A sob follows her out of the room. Hunter doesn't look any better as he clears the table and puts away the leftovers.

"Did Leland really have a date tonight?" Hunter asks when he finishes, sitting at the table with a beer.

Max's shoulders fall. "No. He just… He needs time. I'm asking a lot of him."

"Yeah." Hunter takes a sip of his beer before setting it down. He picks at the label. No one talks. What is there to really say?

"You know—" Hunter laughs, but it's broken and sad. "—after you got better, when we were cleaning out your hospital room, getting ready to bring you home, I found Leland's notebook. The one with the occult stuff. I wondered if he did it, and it worked."

"Occult stuff?" Max asks, his voice shaking around the question.

Hunter's gaze narrows. Max's fingers tighten around mine. I do my best impression of deaf, blind and dumb, but I don't need any clarification. I know exactly what Hunter's talking about.

"Did he?" Hunter's voice is harsh, but also… hopeful. "Did it work? Is that why—"

"Dad," Max's voice is soft—sad enough to have my throat tightening and tears burning the backs of my eyes. "We were kids. And Leland was desperate."

Hunter's shoulders sink. Whatever hope he'd been clinging to, Max just destroyed it. He picks up the beer and drains it. "Are you going to tell Kieran?"

"We should celebrate him getting his ASE first. I don't want to ruin his day. There... There won't be much reason to celebrate for a while after that, so it'll be a happy memory for all of us."

Hunter nods and wipes away a tear before he stands up. "I'm going to help your mother. Give a shout if you need anything."

CHAPTER
EIGHTEEN

MAXTON

The door swings open, slamming against the wall. My best friend stumbles into my room, crashing into the side of my bed with a soft whine. His eyes are red-rimmed and swollen.

Beau grunts and presses against my back, his fingers carefully smoothing over my stomach and up my chest until his palm rests over my still-beating heart.

He's used to Leland—and other members of my family—bursting into our room at all hours of the night. So am I. Neither of us mind, certainly not now that I have days, if not hours, left.

Mom, Dad and Kieran are somewhere in the house, getting rest for the first time in what must be weeks while I struggle to give them a little more time to make peace with my passing. Not that they will—not really, not for a long time.

It's been four months and none of them are even close to being okay, which... can anyone really blame them? My parents are losing a son. My brother is losing his only sibling. And Leland —his best friend for over half his life.

My death is going to destroy them all.

How do you say goodbye to someone you love with every breath you take?

Leland climbs on the bed, carefully moving me over before curling against my chest. He's warm and solid, same as he was when I was sick before. I tuck him under my chin, tossing an arm around his midsection despite the painful rash on my forearm. Beau shuffles closer until I'm surrounded by my two favorite people.

"Promise you'll find me as soon as you get back," Leland whispers into my neck as he reaches up and combs his fingers through my hair.

At least this time I have hair. And eyebrows. Aside from being underweight, and a couple of rashes, I look pretty good all things considered.

"I swear," I say. "As soon as I get back."

He wraps his pinky around mine with a soft sob and I close my eyes, drifting on a sea of nothing for a long, quiet minute.

"He doesn't have long," Beau whispers, his breath hot on my cheek as his gentle hand runs down my side, skipping over the most painful of the rashes but still bumping over every rib on its way to my hip.

"I'll wake everyone," Leland says, pressing his forehead against mine. His breath is hot and rank on my chin. "Love you. See you soon," he whispers, climbing out of bed before I can reply.

He knows; he doesn't need me to say it. Still, I would've liked to tell him how much I love him, that he's the best friend anyone could ever ask for.

His footsteps echo down the hall, and fade.

I pry my eyes open to see Beau hovering over me, eyes sad. My voice is dry and scratchy, lips chapped when I part them. "Kiss for the road?"

Beau cups my cheek. His lips are soft and warm as I breathe the scent of him—something spicy and rich—deep into my lungs.

"I love you," Beau whispers. A wet drop hits my cheek.

"Maxton?" Mom. Dad. Kieran. They're here.

Just in time to say goodbye.

I exhale against Beau's mouth.

When I open my eyes, I'm standing alone in a sea of motionless mist. It clings to every part of me, like a wet blanket. But… not, at the same time. I'm not hot or cold, wet or dry. I just… am.

"Beau?" My voice echoes. "Anyone?"

There's no one—nothing around for miles.

Beau warned me about this.

Lost souls are left adrift in the mist until they are consumed. Or consume another. I need to be quiet and hide. But where?

There's nothing as far as the eye can see. Just the mist. And me.

I turn after several minutes of trying to see *something*, *anything* in the barren landscape, and a red light catches my eye. A soft pulse in the distance. It seems to move closer.

My feet are rooted to the spot even though I know I should run. Beau said to run, to hide, and he'd find me. But I can't move. There's no fear—no panic. Just an ever growing need to find the light. It calls to me.

I take a step forward and the mist bends around me. It feels as if I traveled a hundred miles with a single step. I stumble.

"Easy." A familiar hand slides into mine.

"Beau?" He looks… different, as if I'm looking at myself in a mirror, but seeing myself from someone else's perspective at the same time. Only… not, because he's still himself. I don't understand.

Beau's eyes are still the familiar black with green slits. Horns curl behind his head. And the spider veins that pulse when we make love are ever present. He's himself, more himself than he's ever been, but somehow… more.

"My family?" I ask as I clench his fingers.

Mom. Dad. Kieran. Leland.

Beau squeezes my hand as he pulls me against his chest. He's not warm, or cold. Nor does he smell like... anything. He just is, the same way I am. "Leland is with them."

I frown. "How long has it been?"

I only got here a few minutes ago... right?

"A couple hours," he whispers into my hair.

Hours. It's been hours. My body is cold and stiff by now. Arrangements are most likely being made for my funeral. God. Leland is probably trying his best to hold it together knowing I'll be back, but still losing his shit because I'm gone.

What have I done?

"Max." Beau's voice rolls over me.

I lift my gaze to meet his. "I'm really dead."

Twenty-six years old. And dead.

Too young to die.

Still older than I was ever supposed to get.

Beau wraps his arm around my shoulders and holds me close for another long moment before pulling back. His fingers are gentle as he strokes my cheeks. "We should find a lost soul. Echoes are the easiest to consume. And it's a mercy."

I nod.

A lost soul. Like me.

An echo, so I don't become one myself.

He tugs me forward. This mist parts again.

Suddenly, we're in a valley—sort of. Maybe? The mist still cloaks everything, clinging to my legs, but it seems... different here. Thicker.

I peer into it, trying to find a reason, and shapes begin to form. They're denser, frozen in place, staring at nothing. Vaguely human in shape. Are these... echoes? Is this what I'll become, if I don't consume souls?

Beau's hand curls around my elbow. I glance at him. "They aren't aware of us so they won't fight."

I swallow but… it feels different. As in, I feel nothing. No flex. No tightening of my throat. My mouth isn't dry or wet.

"How…" I look back at the echoes.

"Place your mouth over theirs."

"A kiss?" I have to *kiss* them?

He shakes his head. "Not technically. When you seal a deal as a demon, you consume a portion of the soul you'll collect in full later via mouth. It's how you recognize the soul when the time comes, find it. It's what prevents them from being reborn into another cycle. Humans don't typically feel the loss when a kiss is involved."

I blink. He kissed me when I was a teenager. But… we didn't make a deal for my soul.

Beau's lips twitch into a smile. "Wondering why I kissed you back then?"

"A little."

He shrugs. "I had to make it look real. Leland never would've let me leave if I just agreed without doing *anything*. Plus, it allowed me to transfer the magic necessary for you to heal."

He has a good point. I can't fault his logic.

"So I just…" I look at the echoes once more.

They haven't so much as twitched. It's a little sad. All these souls, cut off from their soul family for eternity, just statues in the mist, waiting to be picked off as they're tortured by the memories of the last life they lived.

"Start here." Beau lays a hand on my back. We shift through the mist and come to a stop in front of one of the echoes. It doesn't acknowledge us, just continues to peer into the distance. I can't tell their gender, age, or what they may have looked like when they were alive. They're just a poor imitation of a human. A stick figure at best. A hazy smoke cloud at worst.

I reach out, pressing my finger into their shoulder.

Nothing. They don't breathe or blink.

Beau's right. This is a fate worse than death.

I lean forward and slot my mouth over theirs. Beau presses against my back, his lips at my ear. "Breathe in."

I suck in a sharp breath and the echo's body wavers before turning into dense smoke. It slides down my throat—thick and kind of sweet, like congealed honey. Not pleasant. But also not the worst thing I've ever eaten.

My fingers and toes tingle. I shake my hands out and look down at them, seeing for the first time I'm not as solid as I feel. Much like the echoes, I'm a poor imitation of a human.

Is this what we are under the flesh and bones? Just a vague outline of thoughts, feelings and memories?

"Keep going," Beau encourages.

"How many do I need?" I ask.

"You'll know when enough is enough."

My gaze travels over the collection of lost souls. I pick one at random and repeat the process. Each time I consume an echo, I feel a sharp ache run through me. It beats almost like my heart did once. A heart I instinctively know I don't have or need any longer.

Beau is beside me the whole time, gently coaxing me to keep going until I stop in front of a small echo.

"It's… a child," I whisper as I reach out and press my fingers to their hair. They aren't any more aware than any of the other echoes.

Beau warned me before, and is proof enough himself—a child can bargain away their soul as easily as an adult. It seems unfair, even cruel that a child can make a deal with a demon.

"I'm surprised they managed to escape the demon they dealt with," Beau says as he squats in front of the echo. "Most don't."

"Is there anything we can do for them?"

I don't like the thought of leaving a child here, even if they don't seem to know where they are or what's happening. Nor do I want to consume them.

Isn't there a way to make this… better?

"Maybe? Souls with unfinished business can return as ghosts. Maybe they could too, if we get them to the gateway."

I frown. "Can you see ghosts?"

It would be cruel to take the child from here and abandon them in a strange world, with no one to help them navigate it, afterwards.

Beau shakes his head. "No. But I bet that witch from The Bone Tarot can. Maybe she can help them."

"How do we get them there?"

They don't seem as if they'll walk of their own free will. Is it possible to drag them after us?

Beau stands and picks the unresponsive child up, slinging them over his shoulder as if they were a sack of potatoes.

I walk beside him, pausing to consume any echo we encounter. And there are plenty. Dozens of lost souls who will never be more than they are now. It's sad, but short of dragging them all to the gateway, which is probably a bad idea, we can't do anything for them.

The further we travel, the more the lost souls thin out. I notice the air around us shimmers a soft purple. Lavender?

I look for the source and—

"Holy shit." I hold my arms out before me. My left forearm, where the worst of the rash used to be… just under the skin, pulsing softly, is a cluster of purple gems of all different sizes. The back of my right hand is the same. I look down and—"I'm naked."

Beau laughs. "What did you expect?"

I don't know what I expected. Not this.

There are more of the same gems on my sides and chest, glowing like a beacon in the mist. A couple of small clusters decorate my thighs and lower leg.

Something brushes against my leg and I swipe out, grabbing it faster than I've ever moved and gasping as a shock travels through my whole body, hitting me right in the balls.

"I have a—" I stare down at the fat oval tip. A purple gem that pulses with an inner light like the others on my body.

"It's cute," Beau says as he grasps the base of my tail, right where it meets my body. I moan and lift onto my toes. "*And sensitive.*"

His smile is wicked as I whimper and twist out of his hold.

CHAPTER
NINETEEN
BEAU

The gateway, as those of us who remember passing through it call the hole in the mist, is nothing like people seem to expect.

For one, it really is just a hole in the mist. A giant opening with a hazy veil distorting the world on the other side. No pearly white gates or old dudes in robes. No winged motherfuckers with burning swords standing nearby, preventing souls from leaving. Souls flow from the exit like water from a mountain spring. Some in groups. Others by themselves. There doesn't seem to be any rhythm or reason to how they leave or who with.

What happens to most souls once they pass through, I don't know. I assume those who are still part of the soul cycle are reborn. Or maybe they pass on to a proper afterlife, where they're temporarily reunited with members of their soul family before being reborn again.

I'll never know what happens to them, or their final destination.

Those who are not reborn, and don't have a chance to reconnect with our soul family—like myself, and Max now—appear near a powerful ley line. It's my hope we pop up in Outer

Banks, but there are similar parahuman settlements built on ley lines scattered around the globe.

I lay my hand on Max's spine, fingers brushing against some of the gems embedded under his off-gray skin, where there used to be a rash caused by the cancer. He shifts into my touch, gasping softly as my fingers slide over the centerpiece of his new demon manifestation.

The purple pulses softly, a pale smoke twisting in the depths. It's like nothing I've ever seen before. He's beautiful—soft gray, covered in purple gems, a matching gem-tipped tail, white horns lined with the same gems that cover his body, and eyes like mine, only purple instead of green. His chin is sharp, cheeks hollow. Inhuman. But it suits him, this new state of being.

Later, I'll take the time to learn exactly how to touch and tease him. Right now, we need to get out of here. But first—

"Close your eyes and remember how you looked as a human to pull your glamor around you. It shouldn't be difficult."

Max closes his eyes. The purple light around him dims before disappearing altogether. He's as I remember him, before the cancer made him sick. As healthy and as handsome as the day I encountered him in the emergency department.

He looks down at his hands, flexing his fingers before his familiar gaze lifts to me. A frown furrows his brow. "It feels weird. Why does it feel weird?"

"It's not who you really are anymore," I explain as I take his hand and squeeze it.

Maxton Grant is dead.

Not… really, not in the sense of truly being dead. He's still here—all the same thoughts, feelings and memories—but the human husk is gone. He's a demon now, and his demon manifestation will always be the most comfortable. Feel the most like… him.

The face of his human life is just the magic masking him the easiest way it knows how. "It'll take some time getting used to the press of magic as it conceals you."

Max runs his hand over his bare chest, and I track the movement, appreciating the sight of him like this just as much as I did him as a demon.

"Now what?" His words draw my attention away from his toned abdomen and soft cock.

"You—sadly—get dressed." I wiggle the bag off my shoulder, the one not currently supporting the weight of a catatonic soul, and Max takes it. He digs inside, pulling out a pair of jeans and a shirt I got from his closet.

Later, when we're home and settled, I'll undress him piece by piece, have him manifest, and explore every change with my tongue. Maybe find out how his new body handles not just one, but two cocks.

"If we get separated on the other side, just focus on Outer Banks—The Bone Tarot to be specific—and the magic will get you there," I tell him once he buttons his pants and smooths his hands down his shirt, tugging out the wrinkles. "Don't panic if you end up somewhere strange." I shift the slight weight on my shoulder as Max nods. "Just try again. The magic is still adjusting to you as much as you are to it, but if you trust it, it'll do exactly what you need and want it to."

It's not more complicated than that.

His magic will work for him, never against him. He won't have to learn how to use it. Most things, he'll just know instinctively after the period of uncertainty passes. Like breathing, I suppose. The magic is a part of him now, tangled with his soul. It's new, weak, but enough to sustain him for the time being.

His eyes drop to the echo over my shoulder as he frowns. "What about them?"

"I'm hoping if I hold on tight enough we'll end up together. If not, I should be able to find them." I won't be able to see or hear them either way, but if they come through with us, the witch from The Bone Tarot should be able to communicate with them.

Max nods. He takes an unnecessary breath before we move as one toward the gateway. Passing through is easy, like stepping from one room and into the next. No pleasant or unpleasant sensation. Nothing to indicate anything is different aside from the sudden influx of sight, sound and sensation. An explosion of life everywhere.

Outer Banks is warm. Parahumans and humans alike walk by, as unconcerned as ever about the two strangers appearing in their midst. We're one of them and that's all that matters.

Before me is the door of The Bone Tarot.

Right next to me is Max.

As for the echo… hopefully they're still with us. I can't see, hear or sense them in any way.

"That was weird," Max mutters.

"What?" I ask.

"Just… it's really that simple?"

"Not usually." It took me a while—what felt like months on the soul plain, but was only a matter of days on earth—to figure out what I needed to do in order to avoid turning into an echo. And that was before I even knew what an echo is.

Then, I stumbled around, consuming souls, until I came across the gateway and slipped through because in my mind anything was better than the endless nothing. It was pure desperation, and a lot of dumb luck, that got me out of the soul plain and back to earth.

Most lost souls don't have anyone there to guide them like Max did, which explains why there are so many echoes.

Scared souls, cut off from everything they know, with no idea what to do next—just frozen in place, by fear and fresh loss.

"Oh—"

The door in front of us is yanked open.

The witch who runs The Bone Tarot glares. It's the first time I've seen her look anything other than pleasant. "Do you have any idea how rude it is to stand aimlessly in public with a wailing child?"

"Oh good. They made it."

She sighs and steps back, pulling the door open further while muttering under her breath and shaking her head. "Bloody bleeding hearts. See if I help next time. Come in." I step forward and she holds up her hand. "Not you. You've got other matters to handle. The kid. Come on, sweetheart. Do you wanna stay with the scary monsters or the nice-looking lady?"

Who is she calling a scary monster?

She doesn't look all that nice right now either.

"Good choice. You're safe now."

The door snaps shut. The lock turns.

I glance at Max, who is peering at me.

Now what?

It's been less than a day since he died. I need to check on his family before they start to wonder where I went. Max can't come though. He can never see his parents or his brother again. Leland, eventually. Possibly tonight, when he's alone. But not right now.

"Max, I…" Shit. It's so unfair.

His face falls and he glances away. "Go. It's okay. They need you a lot more than I do."

"Your papers and phone are on the table at home. Get some rest. I'll text. Okay?"

He nods, eyes downcast, and I lean in, brushing my mouth across his. We knew it would be like this. It still sucks. "I love you."

"I love you," he says. My smile is weak, as weak as his.

I brush my knuckles over his jaw and step back, letting the magic carry me towards the Grant family. I appear in their backyard, hidden behind a cluster of trees Max and I sat under when the weather was still warm, before he was too weak to leave his bed.

It's cold now, thick snow on the ground. Christmas is weeks away but I have a feeling the Grants won't be celebrating this year. Instead, they'll be mourning the death of their eldest son, older brother.

I take my phone from my pocket. It's only been about two hours since I excused myself. It feels as if more time should've passed but no one has ever been able to pin down exactly how time works on the soul plain.

Parahumans have tried.

It's my theory that time on the soul plain works exactly how a soul needs it to. It's unique to each of us. If that really is the case, I'm where I should be, exactly when I should be.

The back door opens, disturbing the cold silence, and Leland steps out, pulling his coat around him. His purple hair lays flat and flops as he runs his fingers through it before collapsing against the wall. When he exhales, his breath fogs the air around his face.

The soft sound of his sobs reaches me and I step out of the shadows, approaching him slowly. He pushes off the wall, stumbling down the stairs, as soon as he notices me.

His voice is a harsh whisper. "Max?"

"Made it back just fine. As soon as you're free…"

I'll take him to Outer Banks. It'll be Leland's first time; Max never got the chance to show him around with me playing chauffeur. Maybe that's for the best. Now Max can show Leland all the places he loves so much as a fresh-faced member of the parahuman community.

Leland rubs at his swollen eyes and wipes his nose with a tissue from his pocket. "The cancer?"

I lay my hand on his shoulder and squeeze. "Gone."

He exhales and nods before clearing his throat and glancing at the house behind him. "We should…"

"How are they?" I ask as we turn towards the back door.

"Heartbroken." Leland's voice trembles.

I give him a moment to gather himself before pushing open the back door.

The house is silent and dark. The air is stale.

It was probably a mistake—Max agreeing to stay here, die here. His parents are going to have to live with his ghost for the rest of their lives. The room he passed away in will become a memorial of sorts. But Max couldn't deny his mother when she asked him if he'd stay.

Leland leads the way deeper into the house.

Hunter, Jill and Kieran are in the living room, huddled together on the sofa. None of them are crying, but their eyes are swollen, glazed over with exhaustion and sadness. They are all a shadow of who they were four months ago.

Cancer killed Max, and destroyed his family along the way.

Not for the first time, I wonder if we did the right thing. Hurting them like this—sharp and deadly like a knife to the heart, instead of a slow bleed out. Would death by a thousand days of fruitless hope be better? Hurt less?

I sit and Leland collapses beside me.

None of us speak.

What is there to say?

CHAPTER TWENTY

This is me now. Maxton Grant—former human, newborn demon.

I finger the glowing purple gems on my side. It should freak me out—this total and complete change—but it doesn't.

Everything, from the white horns encrusted with purple jewels to the tail that seems to have a mind of its own unless I focus on it, just feels like… me. Only, I don't recognize myself.

Will I ever?

"Max?" Beau's voice echoes down the hallway and into the bathroom.

I turn from the mirror, hitting the light as I exit the bathroom and move down the hallway. My tail thumps against my thigh, the feeling new and unfamiliar but somewhat muted by the gym shorts I'm wearing, as I round the corner and come to a halt.

Beau's kicking off his shoes as Leland peers out the windows, eyes wide, lips parted.

Did I look that stupid the first time I took in the view of the mountain range from Beau's apartment window?

Probably.

"You're drooling," I rasp.

Even my voice sounds different. Deeper.

Leland jerks around. His mouth opens and closes like a fish out of water. "Max?"

I run my hand down my chest, rubbing at the gems that pulse with light, suddenly self-conscious. But it's too late to change, and really—why bother?

Leland knows the truth. I'm not human anymore. That part of me is dead. If we're going to keep being best friends, and I fucking hope we do because I don't want to think about losing Leland when I've just lost everyone else, he needs to know all of me just as he always has.

"Hey," I say, "So, uh… I have a tail." I grasp it and pull it around in front of me. "Neat, right?"

A sob tears up Leland's throat as he crosses the short distance between us and throws himself into my arms. I grab him and hold him close as he buries his face in my chest and sobs.

He feels fragile in my arms, as if I could pick him up and throw him across the apartment without breaking a sweat, so I hold him carefully. His fingers bite into my sides. I press my face into his hair and run my hands up and down his shaking back until he calms down.

It takes a while but when the tears subside, he pulls back and rubs at his face before inspecting me. His gaze jumps from one change to another before stopping on the largest cluster of gems on my side.

They run from under my armpit to the waistband of my pants, stretching over my ribs.

Leland presses his fingers to the edge of the patch of jewels. "Is this—" His throat bobs as he swallows. "The rashes, right?"

I lay my hand over top of his. "I think so."

"Does it hurt?"

I shake my head. "No. Nothing hurts. I feel… good. Even better than I did when I was at my healthiest."

He exhales and grins. "The horns and tail are kind of hot. They suit you."

Do they? Or is he just saying that?

"It's going to take some getting used to," I admit as I look at the back of my hand. Even if it all feels right, it still doesn't look that way.

"You will," Beau says, appearing at my side. He holds out a bottle of water to Leland. I accept one as well, even though I'm not thirsty. "Right now, you still feel human, even if you know you're not, so seeing yourself as otherwise is shocking. As the magic settles, and you adjust—" He shrugs. "Most demons forget about their humanity altogether."

Beau never has. It haunts him. Hurts him.

It also makes him who he is, and I love him exactly as he is.

I drop my arm over his shoulder. "I don't want to forget my humanity. Or"—I lift my gaze to Leland—"the best parts of being human."

My family. My best friend.

Leland picks at the label on his water bottle before taking a deep breath. "You said whatever I want. For helping you. I know what I want."

"Okay?" He's had four months to think about it so I'm not surprised. He's not the type to wait to collect either.

"I want to make a deal."

"What?" I gape at him.

Beau shifts against my side and slips his arm around my body. Despite my shock, I notice he's careful to avoid the most sensitive areas.

I'm grateful. I'd rather not pop a boner in front of Leland, who lifts his chin, crosses his arms over his chest and widens his stance. "You heard me."

"What the hell for?" I ask.

He doesn't even know what he's asking.

I never told him what happens to souls that make deals with

demons. It's not something I thought he'd ask for. What the hell could Leland possibly want? I know he's not after power, fame or riches. None of that is his style.

And I swear if he asks for a werewolf boyfriend my parents won't only be planning *my* funeral. I'll strangle him.

"When I die—preferably of old age or other natural causes —I want to become a demon."

"Uh…" I glance at Beau.

Is that even possible? Demons consume the souls they make deals with. But in order for Leland to become a demon, I'd have to… let his soul go. Show him how to consume an echo, the same way Beau showed me.

Am I even capable of making this deal?

"There are some deals demons can't make," Beau says. "A binding contract won't form."

"Why the hell not?" Leland asks.

"When a soul makes a deal with a demon, when the time comes, the demon… consumes the soul. It extends their life and builds their magic," I explain, looking anywhere but at Leland.

I chose this for myself. I don't regret it. Given the choice, I'd do it again, despite all the pain and hardship my choices cause my family. For Leland to know exactly what I chose though… it's not something I ever wanted.

"Because the end result is your soul *not* being consumed, the magic won't attempt to bind it, and thus you'll be put into the soul cycle," Beau says as he strokes my side.

"You still owe me," Leland says, voice low. "And this is what I want."

"I don't know how," I admit. If I did, I'd do it in a heartbeat. The thought of Leland becoming a demon when he's old and finished living his human life, continuing to be my best friend for however long we manage to stick around as demons… I want that. I don't know how.

"Ask for something he can give you," Beau says. We look at

him. "So long as there's a contract, you'll go to the soul plain when you die. Find him and simply choose not to consume him."

A favor bound me and Beau. After he cashed in, a deal made after I got sick is what prevented me from being put into the soul cycle and reborn.

"Okay." I look at Leland. "Something small. I don't think I have enough magic to do anything big yet."

He tips his head back and hums. "Can you make animals— even the mean, abused, have every right to try to eat me, you know what, just *all the animals*—like me? Be kind of nice not to be bitten anymore."

My body warms and magic sparks under my skin. The gems pulse.

"I think so."

"Okay." Leland claps and bounces on his toes. "Let's do this. Pucker up, pretty boy. I have a funeral to plan."

I swallow around the sudden blossom of hurt because I haven't asked Leland about my family. How they're handling my death. Part of me doesn't want to know. I'll ask eventually just… not yet.

"Eager to kiss me?" My smile is forced as I step forward and cup the back of Leland's head. He rolls his eyes and fakes a gag before I slot my mouth over his. His lips part but I refrain from using my tongue and just breathe deep.

I can feel it—his soul—as a small part of it unlatches. When I inhale, it sinks inside of me, becoming part of my magic.

The contract between us is iron clad.

When Leland dies, I'll meet him on the soul plain, help him become a demon. Until then, he's practically a Disney Princess.

"Is that it?" Leland asks when I release him.

I nod and rub my chest. "Yeah. It's done."

"You think it works on shifters?" he asks.

Beau laughs as I glare. Seriously?

"I've never regretted something so fast."

The first thing Leland is going to do is attempt to seduce a hot shifter with his newfound animal charm. Will it work? Who can say? Shifters are part animal so it might. I guess if Leland shows up with a bite taken out of him I'll know.

Leland blows out a sharp breath. "I should get back. Early morning, you know? I just needed to see you for myself."

I open my mouth, close it, and clear my throat. Beau's arm tightens around me and I lean into him. Now. I have to ask now.

"How—" Shit. My voice cracks and I swallow. "How are they?"

My mom, dad and brother.

"Sad." Leland's shoulders fall as he rubs the back of his neck. He seems to curl in on himself and I hate it. He's hurting. "It's going to be a long time before anyone is even remotely okay. Even me."

"Yeah." It's hard to talk around the lump in my throat as I look at my best friend. He looks ten years older than he did four months ago. My slow demise did a number on him.

"But I understand." His smile is weak but real. "This was the better choice for everyone. I'm not mad. It just… My best friend is dead, you know? You're right here, but you're dead too. If that makes any sense."

It makes perfect sense.

I know exactly how he feels.

I'm dead. But I'm not.

"Thank you, Leland. For everything," I whisper.

He's a million in one friend. Without Leland I wouldn't be me. Shit. I wouldn't even be alive. His crazy plan to summon a demon set all of this in motion.

He shrugs. "Until death do us part, right?"

I stride forward and pull him into my arms. "We'll be friends long after death comes for you."

He wraps his arms around me and squeezes hard before pulling back. "I'll see you later this week."

He has to go take care of my family. They need him—his love and support.

I nod and Beau steps forward, grasping Leland's shoulder. He shoots me a small smile before they disappear. My gaze trips around the apartment—Beau's apartment. My apartment.

This is my life now.

And I have zero regrets.

My family will be okay. One day, hopefully when Leland is old and gray after he has lived a full and happy life, I'll meet him on the soul plain and show him how to consume a soul so he can join me here, as a demon.

Until then—

A pair of slender, warm arms wraps around my waist. Beau presses against my back and lays a kiss on my shoulder. "You okay?"

I turn in his arms and bow my head, slotting my mouth over his. His lips part and his tongue meets mine. It splits and I exhale into his mouth as I cup his ass in my hands and pull him close. He rocks against me and smiles into our kiss.

It's been months since we could touch one another in any real way and I'm eager to have him in any way I can.

"Bedroom?" I ask against his mouth.

"Top? Bottom?" he questions as he walks me backwards towards the hallway.

I think about it for a moment. "Why not both?"

TWENTY-ONE
BEAU

E very gasp, moan and whimper from Max only encourages me to keep going until I have four fingers buried knuckle deep in his slick hole. He's so damn tight around the digits, clenching hard enough I'm scared one wrong move will shut this whole thing down.

Not that I'll be mad. That last thing I want to do is hurt Max. If he says stop I will, without hesitation. Now that I have him naked, needy, spread out and mine for the taking I might cry if he puts an end to this. Just, deep on the inside, so he doesn't feel bad. Thankfully, stopping seems to be the last thing on Max's mind.

The gems embedded under his pale skin pulse in the dim light, casting soft shadows on the walls. His tail thumps against the bed—a repeated, uncontrollable motion—every time I withdraw and push my fingers just a little deeper.

Against his stomach, his cock leaks a clear line of fluid. He's not much changed—same length and thickness, but the head is tapered like mine. Pre-cum pools on his belly and I bow my head, licking it away with a soft hum before sucking the head of his cock between my lips.

"Beau!" Max bucks into my mouth, sinking that much deeper.

He's perfect—wild and uncontrolled, a slave to his own desire—and I'm not sure how much control I have left, seeing him like this.

The need to bury myself inside of his body is almost impossible to ignore. I'm barely clinging to my glamor. Without it, my claws will shred his insides.

"I'm close," Max rasps and I pull back, not ready for him to finish yet, even if his recovery time would be minutes, if not seconds. Max groans in frustration, his arms falling to his sides as his tail slaps against my shoulder. "Bastard."

I chuckle under my breath. It's been months since I could touch him, taste him, as more than his dedicated caretaker and what? He thought I was going to rush this? No fucking way.

He glares and I curl my fingers inside of him. The insolent look on his face is instantly replaced by one of desire as his back bows off the mattress and his swollen, wet lips part on a silent moan.

I press my palm to the base of my throbbing cocks and breathe deep before carefully withdrawing my fingers. He's whining, hips rocking, hole gaping.

It's still going to be a tight fit, trying to get both cocks inside him, but not impossible.

My glamor melts away.

"Ready?" My throat is dry as a cooked bone as I smooth my fingers along the inside of Max's thigh, leaving behind faint red lines.

He huffs and grasps behind his knees, pulling his legs to his chest. "Fuck me. Before I push you down and do it myself."

Who am I to argue?

Max knows what he wants, what his body can handle. As a demon, he's not as frail as he was as a human. There's no chance of me tearing him in two. All I have to do is his follow directions and fuck him.

I fist my two cocks, holding them tightly together, and press against his shiny hole. His body opens beautifully, practically sucking me inside. I groan, the sound tangling with Max's low moan of pleasure, as he fists the sheets and tips his hips.

His tail beats a steady rhythm against the mattress as his dark, lust drunk gaze meets mine. Does he have any idea how he looks right now? What the sight of him does to me?

How much I fucking love him?

I grit my teeth and squeeze my eyes shut, doing my best to control the urge to slam into him until every single inch of my cocks is encased by his wet heat. Even if I won't hurt him, I don't want to rush this moment.

This won't be the last time I fuck him like this, but the first time should be savored—enjoyed, like a decadent dessert.

"Beau." Max clamps a clawed hand around my lower arm and his legs curl around my hips. He jerks me forward and I gasp as I plunge into him until his ass presses against my thighs. The sound he makes as his hole flexes around me is pure fucking sin. I shiver and roll my hips, unable to stop myself.

"Fuck. Fuck. You feel—" I don't have the words to describe what it's like to be inside of him like this. My cocks are pressed so tightly together by his body, I can feel the head of one rubbing against the underside of the other. "You okay?"

"Harder." His hand slides up my arm until he's clenching my shoulder. His nails bite into my skin but not hard enough to break flesh.

"Are you—"

"Do it," Max hisses, baring sharp fangs. Purple sparks dance through his eyes. His gems flash bright. I withdraw before slamming into him. The headboard bangs against the wall, and he slides up the mattress as he shouts.

If not for the magical soundproofing, my neighbors would

hear him as I fall into a hard, fast rhythm, fucking him just like he demanded. The bed rocks under us but holds strong—for now. I curl a hand around his shoulder, keeping him in place as I plunge into his body, careful not to ever pull too far out.

"Like that. Beau." He shoves his hand between our bodies. His knuckles drag against my stomach as he pumps his weeping cock and arches his back. I adjust my angle just enough to clasp his hip in my free hand. "Yeah. Yeah. Right there."

Fuck. I'm not going to last.

He needs to blow now.

I bow my head and lick the gems on his side, where the worst of his rash used to be. He cries out, shoving a hand into my hair, nails sharp on my scalp as he tugs the loose strands and continues to pump his cock with the other.

His tail smacks against my side before slipping behind me. I gasp and shiver when it runs down my crease, easily finding my hole and pushing inside.

"Oh, fuck." My hips jerk as my claws bite into his flesh. His tail pushes deeper, the purple gem just the right size and shape to hit the bundle of nerves inside of me.

Max's grin is fucking wicked, all demon, as he fucks me with his tail, pushing me to the brink, as if I wasn't already there. I slot my mouth over his, shoving my tongue between his lips. One of his fangs catches my bottom lip and I taste blood, but don't give a shit as his mouth moves against mine.

Pleasure sparks up my spine. My abdomen clenches as my thighs burn. No fucking way am I going to outlast him. Not at this rate.

"Baby," I whisper against his mouth. "I want to feel you come on my cocks."

He whines, knuckles digging into my flesh as we share breath. "Beau."

Our eyes meet and I press my forehead against his. It's not

just pleasure warming me now, but the all-encompassing love I have for this man too. "Max."

He trembles under me, mouth parting with a silent gasp as wet heat spreads between us. The pressure around my cocks intensifies. It's almost painful, and I gasp. Dark spots dance in my vision as I clench around his tail just as he knocks against my prostate again.

I bury myself inside of him, cocks jerking, cum flooding his insides as I shiver through the rolling waves of pleasure before collapsing on top of him. Max wraps his arms around me, holding me close as I pant against his throat. His breath is warm on my temple; his claws drag softly down my spine. His tail is still inside of me.

"That was…"

I huff and slowly pull out of him. "Yeah."

I sit back on my knees when I think they'll hold my weight and look down, watching as my cum seeps from his hole. He's a mess. I push his thighs further apart before sliding to my belly.

"Beau—" He gasps, jerking his knees up and pressing against my mouth as I lick over his hole before sending my tongue deep inside of him.

He shivers, thighs quivering on either side of my head as I feast—licking, sucking and encouraging every drop of my cum from his body before surging up and claiming his mouth with my own. He moans as our tongues twist together and I share the taste of me with him.

When we finally pull apart, I fall beside him, panting for breath I don't even technically need. Max pulls me close, curling around me as he tucks me under his chin. I close my eyes and rest my head over where his heart used to beat.

There is no soft thump now. Just the steady rise and fall of his chest as he breathes with me. One day in the distant future, he might not even do that.

"Did I do the right thing?" he whispers into my hair.

I run my hand down his side, laying my hand over his pulsing gems. "Only you can decide that, Max."

It's not up to me—to anyone but Max.

He exhales and presses a kiss to my hair. "I love you."

I tip my head back to kiss the underside of his jaw. "I love you."

Even if he wasn't my fated mate, I'd love him. Of that I'm certain.

Today. Tomorrow. Now.

Forever

BONUS STORY

Interested in reading about Leland's HEA? Join my newsletter for a bonus 5k short featuring Leland and a sassy, young shifter who won't take no for an answer.

POSSESSIVE LOVE

To read more books in this series, visit the Possessive Love Amazon page.

ALSO BY ODESSA HYWELL

When you buy direct from Odessa's online shop you save 15% on select items with coupon code BUYDIRECT.

SINFUL DELIGHTS

Always Oskar: Sinful Delights #1

Family Values: Sinful Delights #2

Blood Bound: Sinful Delights #3

Twisted Together

Morally Ambiguous Duet

Say You Love Me: River & Forest

Say You Love Me: Alden & Harrison

Pinewood Lodge

Lovely in Red

For nEver Mine

ABOUT THE AUTHOR

In 2021, Odessa Hywell, a MM romance author decided because she is married to a twin it was best NOT to publish her books featuring twincest and other questionable themes under her married name as her husband would not approve.

—His loss, honestly.—

If you know who Odessa Hywell is, don't be a snitch. Like Benjamin Franklin said, *"Three may keep a secret, if two of them are dead."*

NSFW NEWSLETTER
WWW.ODESSAHYWELL.COM

Printed in Great Britain
by Amazon

37061213R00111